STAR WARS®

EPISODE I

INCREDIBLE CROSS-SECTIONS

WRITTEN BY
DAVID WEST REYNOLDS

ILLUSTRATED BY
HANS JENSSEN
&
RICHARD CHASEMORE

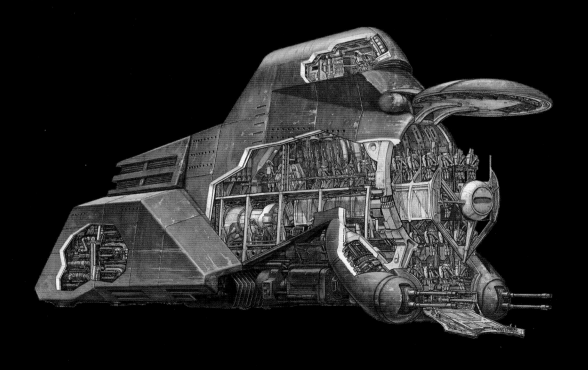

www.starwars.com   LUCAS BOOKS   DK   www.dk.com

CONTENTS

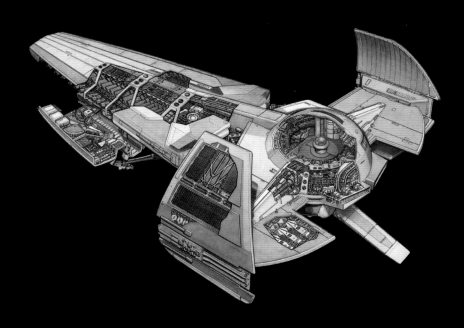

INTRODUCTION

THE VEHICLES OF *Star Wars*: Episode I reveal a time very different from the later day when spacecraft of Empire and Rebels alike will bear the harsh lines and mechanical looks of factory-produced constructions. In this era, the Old Republic still rules the galaxy, and craftsmen still rule the world of design – although in both cases that rule is beginning to unravel. Market forces have only begun to undermine the ancient traditions of craftsmanship, and as a result we see individuality, elegant curves and true art in many of Episodes I's vehicles. Looming over these creations is the spectre of the Trade Federation, with its utilitarian cargo vessels converted into armed war freighters, its greedy practices ready to wipe out the mark of the individual craftsman in the heartless pursuit of profit. For now, however, the galaxy remains filled with extraordinary vessels, testaments – like all things a culture builds – to the unique identity of their age.

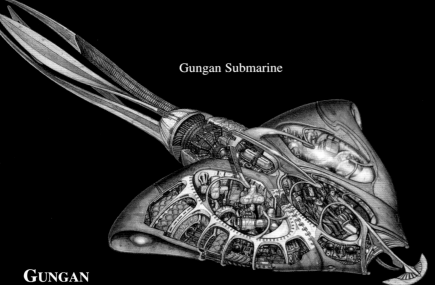

Gungan Submarine

NABOO

The people of the planet Naboo work art into everything they make, dressing their Queen in elaborate finery, building magnificent palaces and cities, and constructing royal space vessels of breathtaking design. Lacking major factories, the Naboo import high-precision components like hyperdrives and sublight engines from major galactic manufacturers on industrialized worlds, but they create beautiful spaceframes and ecologically safe modifications in accordance with the Naboo philosophy of life.

Naboo
N-1 Starfighter

GUNGAN

Quietly conducting their civilization hidden within the swamps and lakes of Naboo, the Gungans create organic artworks and vessels that express their closeness to the rhythms of life. The twin bases of their distinctive designs are the hydrostatic fields, which form bubbles of art in their buildings and submarines, and the organically grown shells they create as the skeletons of their constructions, both produced in a secret manner deep within their underwater cities.

TRADE FEDERATION

The strange society of the Neimoidian traders makes use of a variety of vessels, bearing both the mark of the past and the wave of the future. Their bizarre ground armour is crafted into fearful, vaguely animal-like forms. Their droid starfighters are the high-precision products of a religious culture that will be overrun by the coming of the marketplace. But their war freighters are pure utility, with only traces of the old tradition in their odd configuration. In this harsh texture of armour plate and exposed machinery is the vision of the coming age.

Trade Federation
Droid Starfighter

THE REPUBLIC

Formerly a glorious government of free peoples uniting a vast galaxy in harmony and liberty, the Old Republic has fallen on harder times and has begun cutting back its expenses. As its sky-scraping architecture becomes barren and soulless, so too do its spaceships begin to bear the mark of the factory more than the artist-engineer. Harsh lines and mechanical design distinguish the Republic Cruiser, while many vessels on Coruscant, like the air taxi, still exhibit the older sense of style.

Republic Cruiser

REPUBLIC CRUISER

CARRYING TWO JEDI KNIGHTS into the heart of danger, the Republic Cruiser is dispatched by Supreme Chancellor Valorum to the blockaded planet of Naboo. The direct predecessor to the well-armed Blockade Runner Corvette, the peaceful Republic Cruiser was assembled in the great orbital shipyards of Corellia, and serves as a testament to the quality and fame of Corellian spacecraft design. The *Radiant VII* is a veteran of 34 years in service of the diplomatic corps of Coruscant itself, capital world of the Galactic Republic. The ship has endured many adventures, bringing Jedi Knights, ambassadors and diplomats to trouble spots around the galaxy on missions of security and vital political significance. Its interchangeable salon pods are well-armoured and insulated against any kind of eavesdropping. In this safe haven, critical negotiations can take place and crises can be averted.

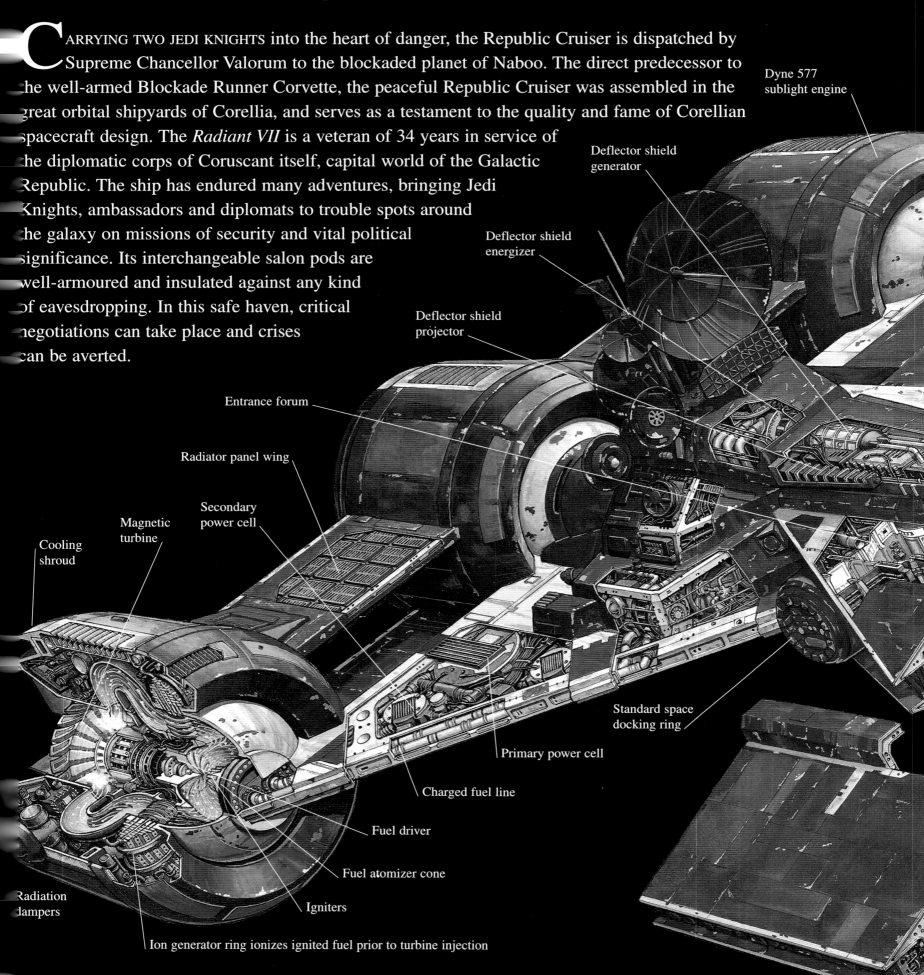

Dyne 577 sublight engine

Deflector shield generator

Deflector shield energizer

Deflector shield projector

Entrance forum

Radiator panel wing

Secondary power cell

Magnetic turbine

Cooling shroud

Radiation dampers

Ion generator ring ionizes ignited fuel prior to turbine injection

Igniters

Fuel atomizer cone

Fuel driver

Charged fuel line

Primary power cell

Standard space docking ring

8-person escape pod

COLOUR SIGNAL

The striking red colour of the Republic Cruiser sends a message to all who see it. Scarlet declares the ship's diplomatic immunity and serves as a warning not to attack. Red is the colour of ambassadorial relations and neutrality for spacecraft of the Galactic Republic, and has been for generations. The tradition will continue even into the days of the Empire: Princess Leia Organa's consular vessel *Tantive IV* of Alderaan is striped in red to indicate its special diplomatic status. The extraordinary full-red colour scheme of the Republic Cruiser signifies that the ship comes straight from the great capital world of Coruscant.

THE SALON POD

The Republic Cruiser often serves as a neutral meeting ground for Republic officials and leaders of groups in conflict. To accommodate the many kinds of alien physiology in the galaxy, customized salon pods are available in the hangars on Coruscant, and the Republic Cruiser can be equipped with any of these. In emergency situations, the entire salon pod can eject from the cruiser with its own sensors and independent life-support gear ready to sustain the diplomatic party on board.

COMMUNICATING IN A DIVERSE GALAXY

In order to communicate with any culture it may visit, the Republic Cruiser sports a wide variety of dish and other communications antennas. (Years later, the Empire will standardize communications across the galaxy, making such an array unnecessary.) On board the cruiser, two communications officers specialize in operating the communication computers, deciphering strange languages and decoding the complex signal pulses of unorthodox alien transmissions.

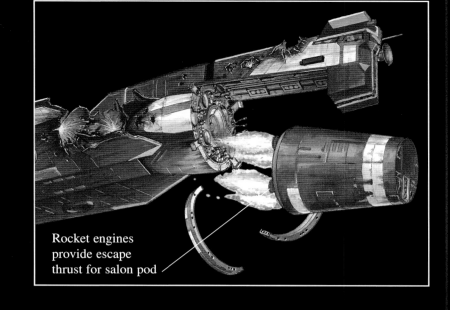

Rocket engines provide escape thrust for salon pod

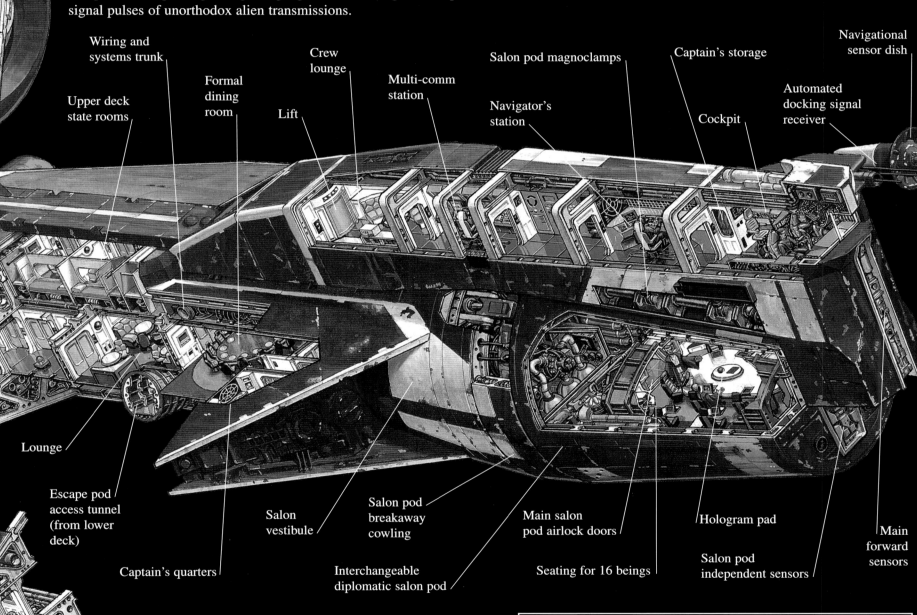

Wiring and systems trunk

Upper deck state rooms

Formal dining room

Crew lounge

Lift

Multi-comm station

Salon pod magnoclamps

Navigator's station

Captain's storage

Cockpit

Navigational sensor dish

Automated docking signal receiver

Lounge

Escape pod access tunnel (from lower deck)

Captain's quarters

Salon vestibule

Salon pod breakaway cowling

Interchangeable diplomatic salon pod

Main salon pod airlock doors

Seating for 16 beings

Hologram pad

Salon pod independent sensors

Main forward sensors

Mid-deck corridor

Droid hold

TIGHT SECURITY

Civilian models of the Corellian Cruiser are used for straightforward transport purposes, but the scarlet Republic Cruisers are dedicated to the special objectives of galactic political service. To accomplish their missions, Republic Cruisers must often rely on their reputation as absolutely secure vessels for high-level diplomatic meetings and confrontations. For security reasons, crew is kept to a bare minimum, with many ship functions attended by simple utility droids.

DATA FILE

Manufacturer: Corellian Engineering Corporation
Make: Space Cruiser
Length: 115 m (380 ft)
Sublight engines: 3 Dyne 577 radial atomizers
Hyperdrive: Longe Voltrans tri-arc CD-3.2
Crew: 8 (captain, 2 co-pilots, 2 communications officers, 3 engineers)
Passenger capacity: 16
Armament: none (unarmed diplomatic vessel)
Escape pods: two 8-person pods plus salon pod

LANDING SHIP

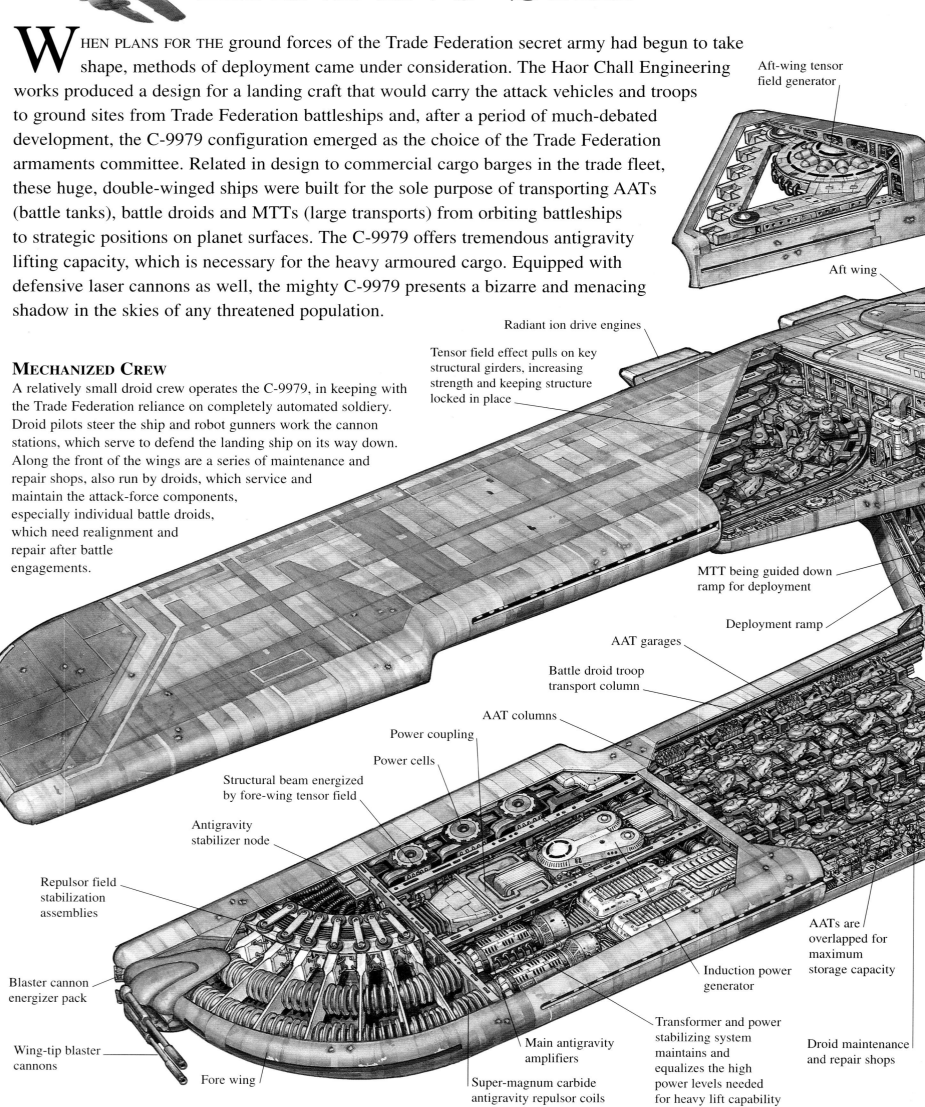

WHEN PLANS FOR THE ground forces of the Trade Federation secret army had begun to take shape, methods of deployment came under consideration. The Haor Chall Engineering works produced a design for a landing craft that would carry the attack vehicles and troops to ground sites from Trade Federation battleships and, after a period of much-debated development, the C-9979 configuration emerged as the choice of the Trade Federation armaments committee. Related in design to commercial cargo barges in the trade fleet, these huge, double-winged ships were built for the sole purpose of transporting AATs (battle tanks), battle droids and MTTs (large transports) from orbiting battleships to strategic positions on planet surfaces. The C-9979 offers tremendous antigravity lifting capacity, which is necessary for the heavy armoured cargo. Equipped with defensive laser cannons as well, the mighty C-9979 presents a bizarre and menacing shadow in the skies of any threatened population.

MECHANIZED CREW

A relatively small droid crew operates the C-9979, in keeping with the Trade Federation reliance on completely automated soldiery. Droid pilots steer the ship and robot gunners work the cannon stations, which serve to defend the landing ship on its way down. Along the front of the wings are a series of maintenance and repair shops, also run by droids, which service and maintain the attack-force components, especially individual battle droids, which need realignment and repair after battle engagements.

Aft-wing tensor field generator

Aft wing

Radiant ion drive engines

Tensor field effect pulls on key structural girders, increasing strength and keeping structure locked in place

MTT being guided down ramp for deployment

Deployment ramp

AAT garages

Battle droid troop transport column

AAT columns

Power coupling

Power cells

Structural beam energized by fore-wing tensor field

Antigravity stabilizer node

Repulsor field stabilization assemblies

Blaster cannon energizer pack

Wing-tip blaster cannons

Fore wing

Main antigravity amplifiers

Super-magnum carbide antigravity repulsor coils

Induction power generator

Transformer and power stabilizing system maintains and equalizes the high power levels needed for heavy lift capability

AATs are overlapped for maximum storage capacity

Droid maintenance and repair shops

LOADING

C-9979 landing ships are berthed in hidden hangar areas of the Trade Federation battleships. Here they are assembled, serviced and maintained, and when ready for deployment they are loaded with MTTs, AATs and troop carriers which have been prepared for combat. Landing ships are stored in an unloaded condition to reduce structural stress and so that the attack craft can be serviced individually.

DATA FILE

Design and manufacture: Haor Chall Engineering
Wingspan: 370 m (1,200 ft)
Hyperdrive: none
Max. atmospheric speed: 587 kph (365 mph)
Troop carrier capacity: 7 per wing; total 28
AAT (battle tank) capacity: 24 per fore wing, 33 per aft wing; total 114
MTT (large transport) capacity: 3 per fore wing, 3 in stage area, 2 in landing pedestal; total 11
Crew: 88 (droids only)
Armament: 2 pairs of wing-tip laser cannons, 4 turret-mounted cannons

Electromagnetic transport clamp-on rail will guide MTT down deployment ramp

Control centre

MTT powers up its onboard repulsors in staging area

Control signal receiver picks up vital signal from the Droid Control Ship

Deflector shield projectors

Pressure charging turbine atmosphere intake

Cannon charging turret

Main defensive cannon

Wing-tip plating is an alloy composite transparent to repulsor effect

Fore-wing tensor field generator

Radiator panel for tensor power system

Navigation sensors

Combat sensors

Forward tensor field generator increases load-bearing ability of wing mounts

Staging area

MTT garage

Antigravity rails support MTTs

Centre MTT has deployed and an AAT now follows into position

Main deployment doors include perimeter field sensors to detect possible land mines, electrical fields and other hazards

Doors require clear landing area for opening clearance

Landing gear fairing

MTT preparing to back into position over deployment ramp

Foot ramp

Atmosphere pressure charging turbines

Tanks in escort position

MTT moving out for battle position

DEPLOYMENT

The wings of the landing ship contain rows of MTTs, AATs and battle droid troop carriers racked in garage channels for maximum loading capacity. For deployment, the attack vehicles are guided along repulsor tracks to a staging platform. MTTs in particular require the assistance of the repulsors built into these tracks, because their onboard manoeuvring equipment is not precise enough to negotiate the cramped confines of the garage zones without causing collision damage. At a staging platform, the vehicles are rotated into position and seized by transport clamps, which draw them aft and guide them down the drop ramp in the landing ship's "foot". The great clamshell doors of the "foot" then open wide to release the ground forces. Deployment of the full load of vehicles on board a C-9979 can take up to 45 minutes.

STORING THE TRANSPORT

C-9979s are built with removable wings so they can be stored efficiently. Powerful tensor fields bind the wings to the fuselage when the ship is assembled for use. The huge wings of the C-9979 would tax the load-bearing capabilities of even the strongest metal alloys, making tensor fields vital for the integrity of the ship. Forward-mounted tensor fields bind the wing mounts firmly to the fuselage, while wing-mounted tensor fields keep the span of the wings from sagging.

MTT (LARGE TRANSPORT)

DATA FILE
Design and manufacture: Baktoid Armour Workshop
Troop capacity: 112 battle droids carrying standard blaster rifles
Armament: four 17 kv anti-personnel blasters twin-mounted in ball turrets
Length: 31 m (103 ft)
Height: 13 m (43 ft)
Max. ground speed: 35 kph (22 mph)
Max. lift altitude: 4 m (13 ft)
Deployment method: carried to planet surface in C-9979 landing ship

THE TRADE FEDERATION'S Baktoid Armour Workshop has long designed armaments for Trade Federation customers. When called upon to design and build vehicles for the Trade Federation droid army, it easily turned its resources to the creation of deadly weapons made to ensure a long line of future customers. The Trade Federation MTT (Multi-Troop Transport, or simply large transport) was designed to convey platoons of ground troops to the battlefield and support them there. Its deployment on Naboo is its first use in major military action, and many large transports had seen only training exercises on remote worlds before being used there. They are designed for deployment in traditional battle lines, hence their heavy frontal armour. Reinforced and studded with case-hardened metal alloy studs, the MTT's face is designed to ram through walls so that troops may be deployed directly into enemy buildings (or "future customer buildings", as the Trade Federation often prefers to say). When ready to deploy, it opens its large front hatch to release the battle droid contingents from its huge storage rack, extended on a powerful hydraulic rail. Two droid pilots direct it according to instructions transmitted from the orbiting Droid Control Ship.

Control room escape hatch (at rear)

Lift

Repulsorlift sled

Drive unit adapted from civilian cargo sled

Deployment rack extensor drive

Rack operator droid

Rack drive heat exhaust vents

Rack extensor drive engine

Pressure equalizer valves

TROOP CARRIER

The Trade Federation troop carrier conveys battle droid units to deployment zones behind the protection of ground armour, in secure conditions, or within occupied areas. A rack similar to that in the MTT contains a full complement of 112 battle droids folded into their space-saving configuration, ready for action on release.

Power converter grids

HEAVY LIFTING

The MTT's engine works hard to power repulsorlifts that carry a very heavy load of troops and solid armour. The repulsorlift generator's exhaust and cooling system is vented straight down towards the ground through several large vents under the vehicle. This creates a billowing storm of wind around the MTT, which lends it a powerful and menacing air.

Kuat Premion Mk. II power generators

Repulsor motor gas cooling system exhaust

Heavy-duty repulsor cooling fins

THE BAKTOID SIGNATURE IN DESIGN

The MTT (large transport) was designed by the same Baktoid workshop that developed the AAT (battle tank) for the Trade Federation secret army. The distinctive Baktoid style gives both vehicles a look reminiscent of heavy, jungle-dwelling animals. Both are designed for use in formal battle lines and place vital equipment such as reactor and main engines at the rear, protected behind the heavy armour of the front surfaces.

THE DEPLOYMENT RACK

The original design of the MTT called for an open staging chamber inside it, but the Baktoid Armour Workshop is known for its original designs, and the MTT had the unusual job of conveying soldiers that were not living beings, but droids. The Baktoid engineers worked out a system that would load battle droids folded into very small configurations into a giant deployment rack. This rack would more than double the troop capacity of the MTT, extending to release the compressed troops which would then unfold into fighting configuration. At the conclusion of a battle, troops are reloaded into the rack and safely carried back to their base. The original open-staging chamber MTT design was retained for carrying wheel-like destroyer droids.

Control signal receiver

Control room

Battle droid pilot

Battle droid engineer/gunner

Main troop deployment hatch

Droid guns stored on backpacks

Droid soldiers racked in compressed form for maximum capacity

Troop deployment rack extends to release droid soldiers

Overseer catwalk

Battle droids unfold to combat stance when deployed

Lower troop deployment hatch

Twin blaster cannons in ball turrets

Laser power capacitor

Laser power modulator

Heavy forward armour

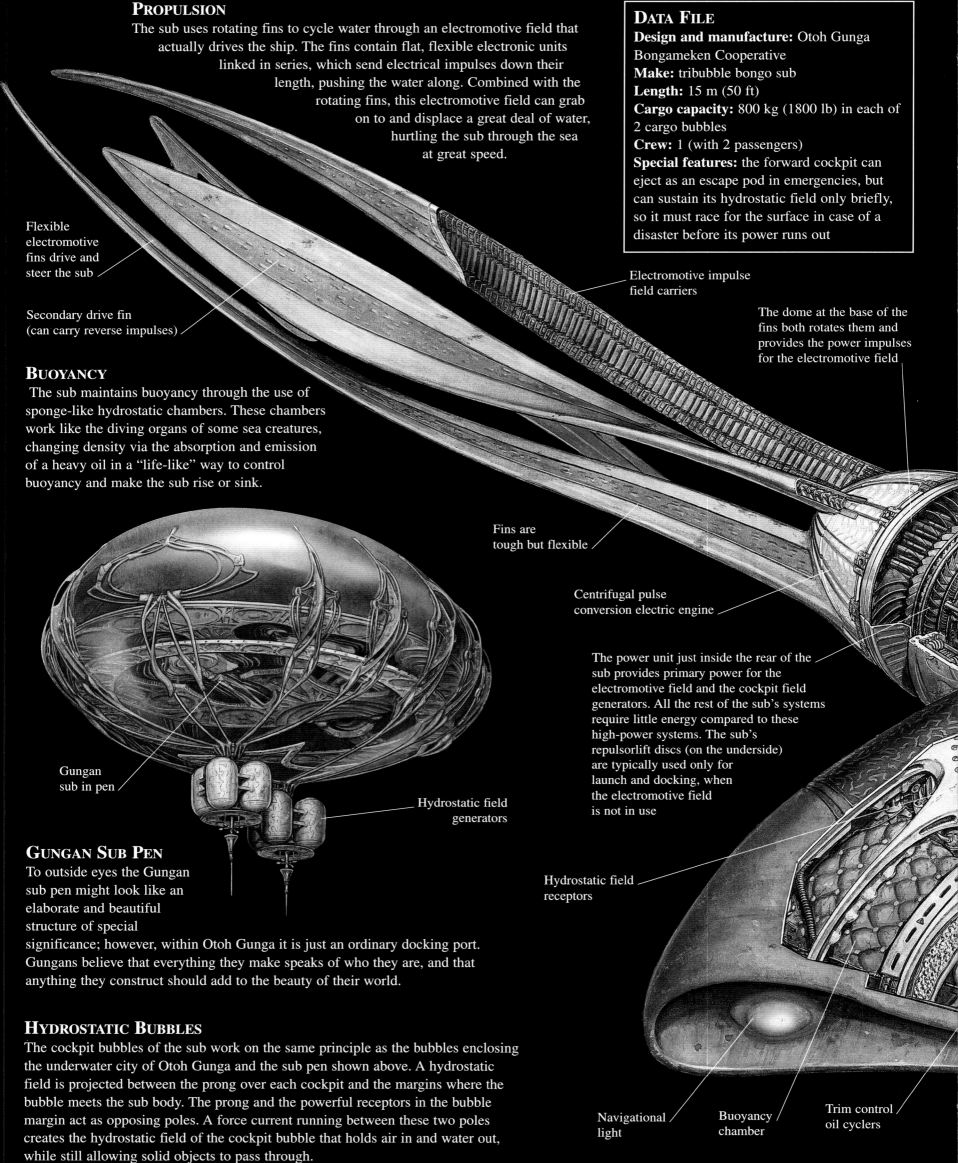

PROPULSION

The sub uses rotating fins to cycle water through an electromotive field that actually drives the ship. The fins contain flat, flexible electronic units linked in series, which send electrical impulses down their length, pushing the water along. Combined with the rotating fins, this electromotive field can grab on to and displace a great deal of water, hurtling the sub through the sea at great speed.

DATA FILE
Design and manufacture: Otoh Gunga Bongameken Cooperative
Make: tribubble bongo sub
Length: 15 m (50 ft)
Cargo capacity: 800 kg (1800 lb) in each of 2 cargo bubbles
Crew: 1 (with 2 passengers)
Special features: the forward cockpit can eject as an escape pod in emergencies, but can sustain its hydrostatic field only briefly, so it must race for the surface in case of a disaster before its power runs out

Flexible electromotive fins drive and steer the sub

Secondary drive fin (can carry reverse impulses)

Electromotive impulse field carriers

The dome at the base of the fins both rotates them and provides the power impulses for the electromotive field

BUOYANCY

The sub maintains buoyancy through the use of sponge-like hydrostatic chambers. These chambers work like the diving organs of some sea creatures, changing density via the absorption and emission of a heavy oil in a "life-like" way to control buoyancy and make the sub rise or sink.

Fins are tough but flexible

Centrifugal pulse conversion electric engine

The power unit just inside the rear of the sub provides primary power for the electromotive field and the cockpit field generators. All the rest of the sub's systems require little energy compared to these high-power systems. The sub's repulsorlift discs (on the underside) are typically used only for launch and docking, when the electromotive field is not in use

Gungan sub in pen

Hydrostatic field generators

GUNGAN SUB PEN

To outside eyes the Gungan sub pen might look like an elaborate and beautiful structure of special significance; however, within Otoh Gunga it is just an ordinary docking port. Gungans believe that everything they make speaks of who they are, and that anything they construct should add to the beauty of their world.

Hydrostatic field receptors

HYDROSTATIC BUBBLES

The cockpit bubbles of the sub work on the same principle as the bubbles enclosing the underwater city of Otoh Gunga and the sub pen shown above. A hydrostatic field is projected between the prong over each cockpit and the margins where the bubble meets the sub body. The prong and the powerful receptors in the bubble margin act as opposing poles. A force current running between these two poles creates the hydrostatic field of the cockpit bubble that holds air in and water out, while still allowing solid objects to pass through.

Navigational light

Buoyancy chamber

Trim control oil cyclers

GUNGAN SUB

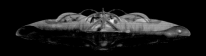

THIS KIND OF SUBMERSIBLE is a common utility transport in Otoh Gunga, designed to carry passengers, cargo or both. The forward cockpit bubble carries only pilot and passengers, but the side bubbles can carry either passengers or cargo depending on whether they are fitted with seats. The sub's distinctive form originates from both the Gungans' construction methods and their love of artistic design. The Gungans produce many of their structures using a secret method that actually "grows" the basic skeletons or shells of buildings or vehicles. This gives Gungan constructions a distinctive organic look, which is then complemented by artistic detail, even on simple vehicles like the sub. Gungan organically generated shells can be combined to make complex constructions, and then modified and fitted with electronic and mechanical components to give them the needed functionality. The organic skeletons are exceptionally strong, though still susceptible to damage by some of the larger sea monsters encountered in deep waters.

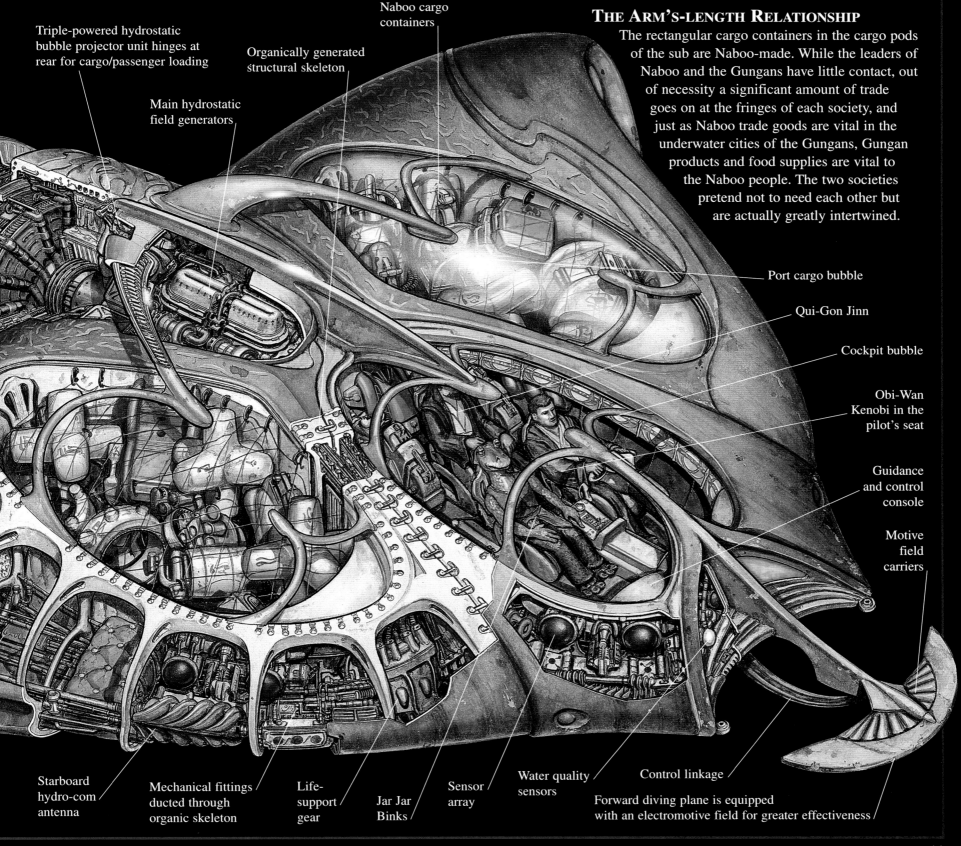

Triple-powered hydrostatic bubble projector unit hinges at rear for cargo/passenger loading

Main hydrostatic field generators

Organically generated structural skeleton

Naboo cargo containers

THE ARM'S-LENGTH RELATIONSHIP

The rectangular cargo containers in the cargo pods of the sub are Naboo-made. While the leaders of Naboo and the Gungans have little contact, out of necessity a significant amount of trade goes on at the fringes of each society, and just as Naboo trade goods are vital in the underwater cities of the Gungans, Gungan products and food supplies are vital to the Naboo people. The two societies pretend not to need each other but are actually greatly intertwined.

Port cargo bubble

Qui-Gon Jinn

Cockpit bubble

Obi-Wan Kenobi in the pilot's seat

Guidance and control console

Motive field carriers

Starboard hydro-com antenna

Mechanical fittings ducted through organic skeleton

Life-support gear

Jar Jar Binks

Sensor array

Water quality sensors

Control linkage

Forward diving plane is equipped with an electromotive field for greater effectiveness

NABOO QUEEN'S ROYAL STARSHIP

THE ROYAL STARSHIP of Queen Amidala of Naboo is a unique starship handcrafted by the Theed Palace Space Vessel Engineering Corps. Completed six years ago, the Royal Starship replaced the previous royal vessel before Queen Amidala came to office. The gleaming craft, usually helmed by the Queen's chief pilot Ric Olié, conveys Queen Amidala in matchless style to locations around Naboo for royal visitations, parades and other observances. The ship also carries Amidala on formal state visits to other planetary rulers or to the Galactic Senate at the capital world of Coruscant itself. It is designed for short trips and accordingly features limited sleeping facilities, primarily dedicated for the ruler and a customary entourage.

Expressing the Naboo love of beauty and art, the dream-like shape of the Queen's ship, together with its extraordinary chromium finish, make it a distinctive presence in any setting. The starship is made to embody the glory of the Naboo royalty, symbol of the noble spirit of the Naboo people. Service to the Queen is a great honour, and the design of a Royal Starship is the highest goal to which a Naboo engineer can aspire. Every centimetre of the ship's wiring is laid out with exacting precision, neatly run in perfect parallel rows, making the ship a work of art in every respect.

ROYAL CHROMIUM

A mirrored chromium finish gleams over the entire surface of the Royal Starship from stem to stern. Purely decorative, this finish indicates the starship's royal nature. Only the Queen's own vessel may be entirely chromed. Royal starfighters are partly chromed, and non-royal Naboo ships bear no chrome at all. The flawless hand-polished chrome surface over the entire Royal Starship is extremely difficult to produce and is executed by traditional craftspeople, not by factory or droid equipment.

NUBIAN AT HEART

The starship's unique spaceframe was manufactured at Theed, yet the ship makes use of many standard galactic high-technology components that cannot be produced on Naboo. The ship is built around elegant Nubian 327 sublight and hyperdrive propulsion system components, giving it high performance and an exotic air. Nubian systems are often sought by galactic royalty and discriminating buyers who appreciate the distinctive design flair of Nubian components. Nubian equipment is easily acquired on civilized worlds but can be hard to obtain on more remote planets, as the Queen discovers during her forced landing on Tatooine.

Starboard sensor array dome

Main hold

Tech station

Jar Jar Binks

Lift to lower deck

Table

Hyperdrive bay (in floor)

Forward hold

Royal quarters

Navigation light recess

Extension boarding ramp to lower deck

Navigation floodlight

Forward maintenance station

Wiring throughout the ship is laid out with exacting care and precision to honour the Queen

Power node

Communications antennas

Forward bulkhead

Forward long-range sensor array

Navigational sensors

Forward deflector shield projector

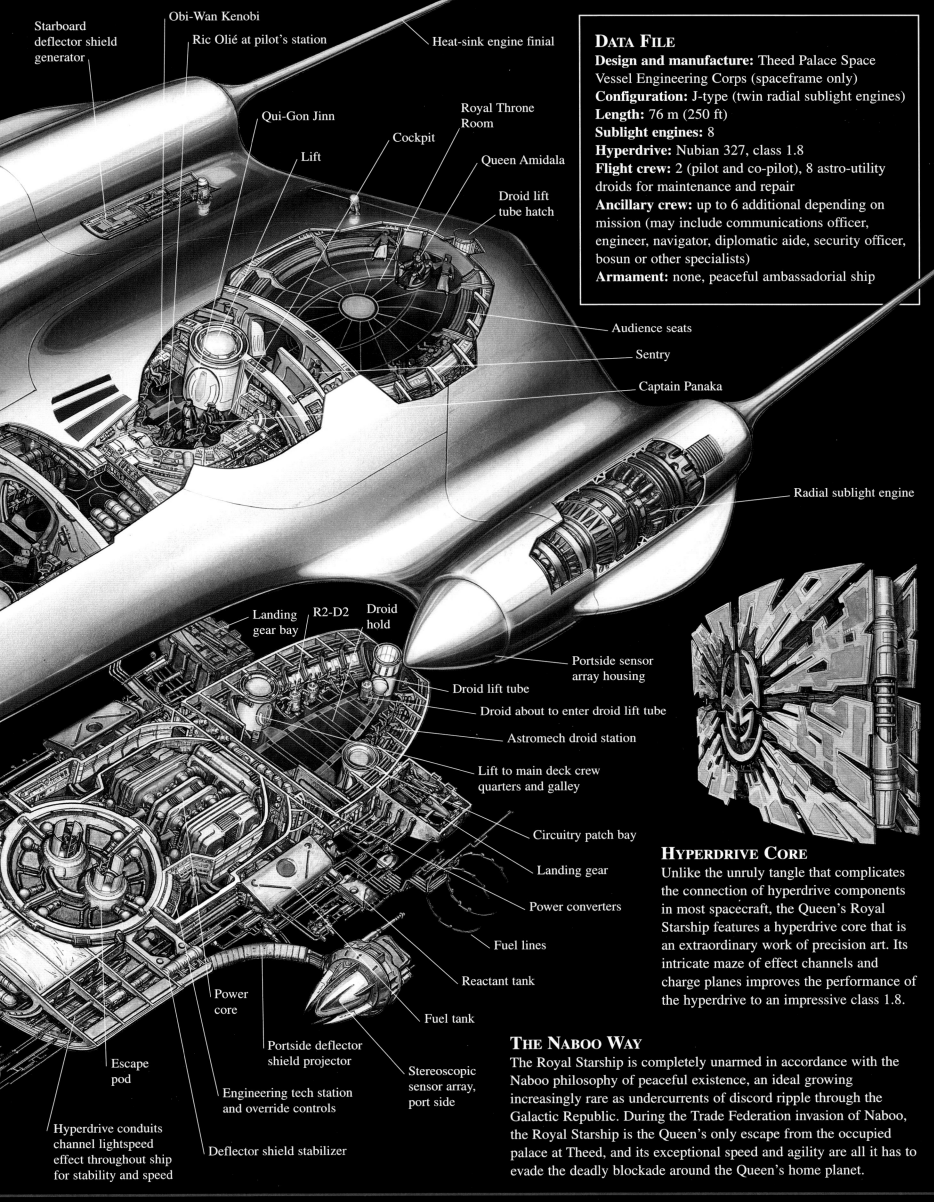

Starboard deflector shield generator

Obi-Wan Kenobi

Ric Olié at pilot's station

Heat-sink engine finial

Qui-Gon Jinn

Royal Throne Room

Cockpit

Lift

Queen Amidala

Droid lift tube hatch

DATA FILE
Design and manufacture: Theed Palace Space Vessel Engineering Corps (spaceframe only)
Configuration: J-type (twin radial sublight engines)
Length: 76 m (250 ft)
Sublight engines: 8
Hyperdrive: Nubian 327, class 1.8
Flight crew: 2 (pilot and co-pilot), 8 astro-utility droids for maintenance and repair
Ancillary crew: up to 6 additional depending on mission (may include communications officer, engineer, navigator, diplomatic aide, security officer, bosun or other specialists)
Armament: none, peaceful ambassadorial ship

Audience seats

Sentry

Captain Panaka

Radial sublight engine

Landing gear bay

R2-D2

Droid hold

Portside sensor array housing

Droid lift tube

Droid about to enter droid lift tube

Astromech droid station

Lift to main deck crew quarters and galley

Circuitry patch bay

Landing gear

Power converters

Fuel lines

Reactant tank

Power core

Fuel tank

Escape pod

Portside deflector shield projector

Stereoscopic sensor array, port side

Engineering tech station and override controls

Hyperdrive conduits channel lightspeed effect throughout ship for stability and speed

Deflector shield stabilizer

HYPERDRIVE CORE
Unlike the unruly tangle that complicates the connection of hyperdrive components in most spacecraft, the Queen's Royal Starship features a hyperdrive core that is an extraordinary work of precision art. Its intricate maze of effect channels and charge planes improves the performance of the hyperdrive to an impressive class 1.8.

THE NABOO WAY
The Royal Starship is completely unarmed in accordance with the Naboo philosophy of peaceful existence, an ideal growing increasingly rare as undercurrents of discord ripple through the Galactic Republic. During the Trade Federation invasion of Naboo, the Royal Starship is the Queen's only escape from the occupied palace at Theed, and its exceptional speed and agility are all it has to evade the deadly blockade around the Queen's home planet.

PODRACERS

HﾍGH-SPEED PODRACING hearkens back to primitive eras with its traditional Podracer designs and the mortal danger seen in racing spectacles. Pulled on flexible control cables by fearsomely powerful independent engines, a small open cockpit (the "Pod") carries a daring pilot at speeds that can exceed 800 kilometres (500 miles) per hour. Considered in its lightning-fast modern form too much for humans to manage, Podracing is almost exclusively carried on by other species that sport more limbs, more durable bodies, a wider range of sensory organs or other biological advantages.

TEEMTO'S PODRACER

Teemto Pagalies' Podracer is typical of Podracers found in the Outer Rim: a unique design incorporating certain standard features. Its unusual circular shape is designed around an internal metal cycling ring which acts as a gyroscopic stabilizer for the non-aerodynamic Pod. Other components are standard: control line anchors, a brace of repulsors to float the Podracer safely off the ground, a complex engine sensor and telemetry computer package, and a variety of control levers and switches suited to the particular body shape of the race pilot himself.

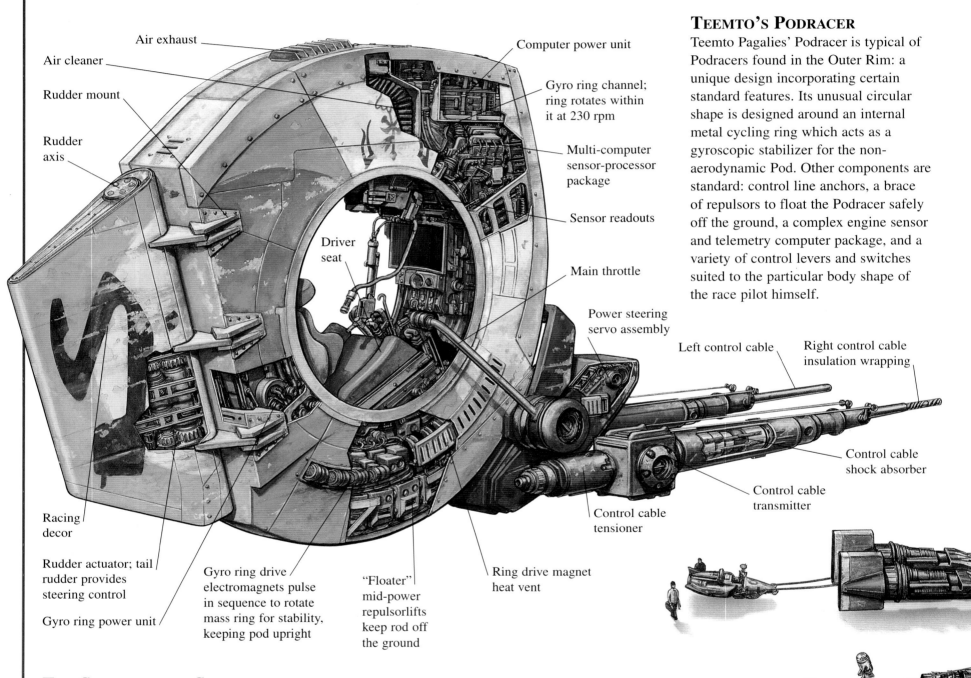

Air exhaust

Air cleaner

Rudder mount

Rudder axis

Computer power unit

Gyro ring channel; ring rotates within it at 230 rpm

Multi-computer sensor-processor package

Sensor readouts

Driver seat

Main throttle

Power steering servo assembly

Left control cable

Right control cable insulation wrapping

Control cable shock absorber

Control cable transmitter

Racing decor

Rudder actuator; tail rudder provides steering control

Gyro ring power unit

Gyro ring drive electromagnets pulse in sequence to rotate mass ring for stability, keeping pod upright

"Floater" mid-power repulsorlifts keep rod off the ground

Ring drive magnet heat vent

Control cable tensioner

THE STORY OF THE SPORT

Podracing has its origins in ancient contests of animal-drawn carts, of the kind still seen in extremely primitive systems far from the space lanes. Long ago a daring mechanic called Phoebos recreated the old arrangement with repulsorlift Pods and flaming jet engines for a whole new level of competition and risk. The famous first experimental race ensured Podracing's reputation as an incredibly dangerous and popular sport.

PODRACING TODAY

Long ago banned from most civilized systems, Podracing is still famous on Malastare and in a few other locales. Real Podracing aficionados, however, look beyond the Republic to the rugged worlds of the Outer Rim, where Podraces still serve as a spectacle for hundreds of thousands and vast gambling fortunes are made and lost. This naturally makes the Hutts an accessory to most racing venues.

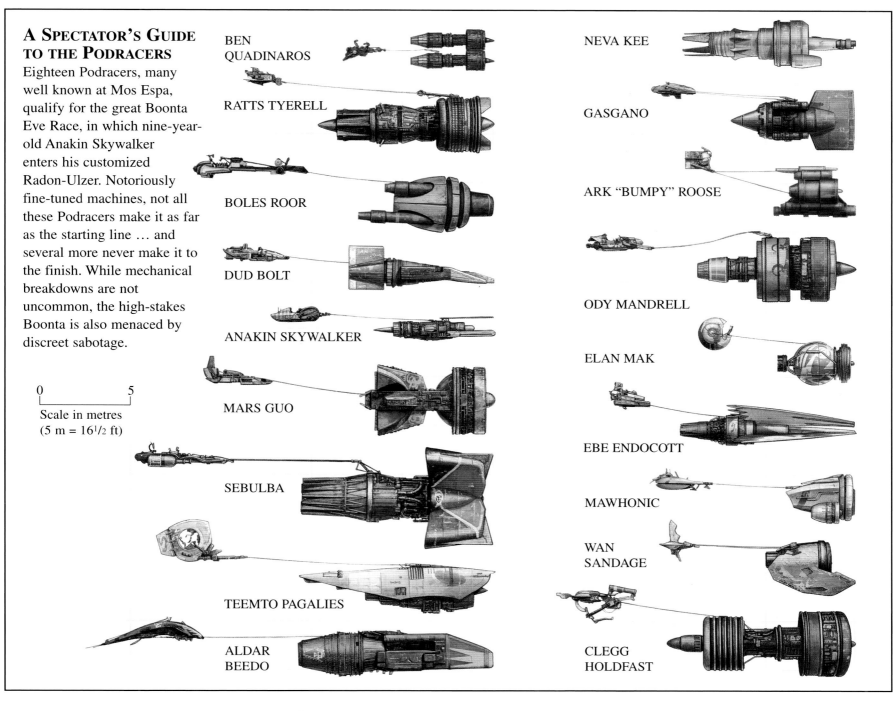

A Spectator's Guide to the Podracers

Eighteen Podracers, many well known at Mos Espa, qualify for the great Boonta Eve Race, in which nine-year-old Anakin Skywalker enters his customized Radon-Ulzer. Notoriously fine-tuned machines, not all these Podracers make it as far as the starting line … and several more never make it to the finish. While mechanical breakdowns are not uncommon, the high-stakes Boonta is also menaced by discreet sabotage.

0 ———— 5

Scale in metres
(5 m = 16$\frac{1}{2}$ ft)

BEN QUADINAROS

RATTS TYERELL

BOLES ROOR

DUD BOLT

ANAKIN SKYWALKER

MARS GUO

SEBULBA

TEEMTO PAGALIES

ALDAR BEEDO

NEVA KEE

GASGANO

ARK "BUMPY" ROOSE

ODY MANDRELL

ELAN MAK

EBE ENDOCOTT

MAWHONIC

WAN SANDAGE

CLEGG HOLDFAST

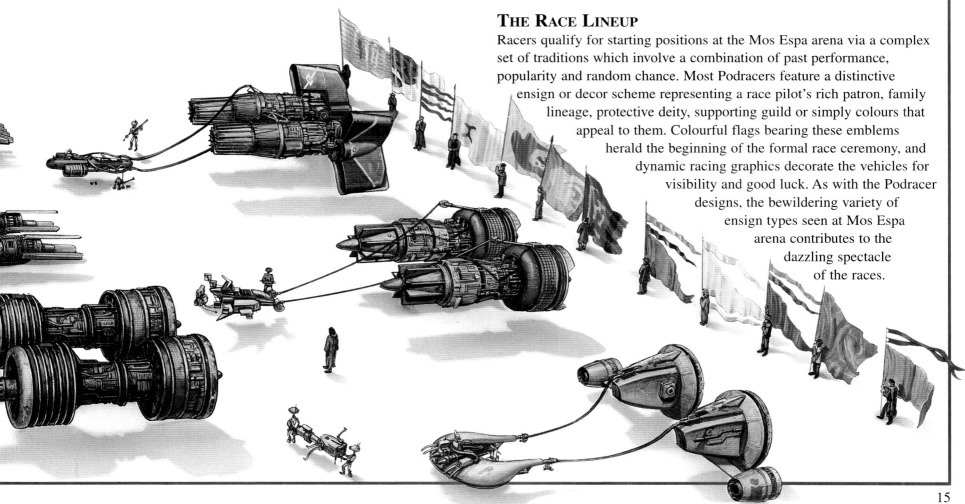

The Race Lineup

Racers qualify for starting positions at the Mos Espa arena via a complex set of traditions which involve a combination of past performance, popularity and random chance. Most Podracers feature a distinctive ensign or decor scheme representing a race pilot's rich patron, family lineage, protective deity, supporting guild or simply colours that appeal to them. Colourful flags bearing these emblems herald the beginning of the formal race ceremony, and dynamic racing graphics decorate the vehicles for visibility and good luck. As with the Podracer designs, the bewildering variety of ensign types seen at Mos Espa arena contributes to the dazzling spectacle of the races.

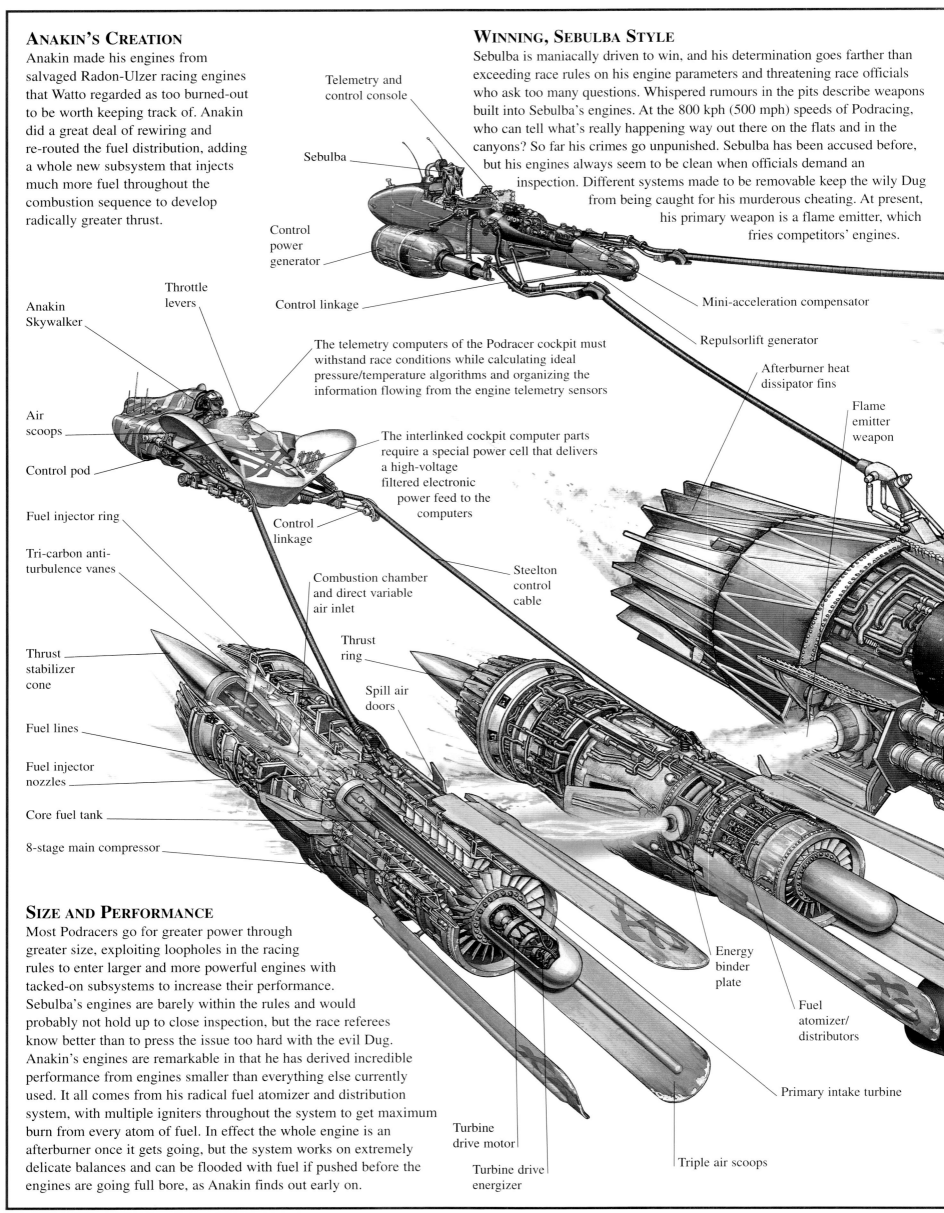

ANAKIN'S CREATION

Anakin made his engines from salvaged Radon-Ulzer racing engines that Watto regarded as too burned-out to be worth keeping track of. Anakin did a great deal of rewiring and re-routed the fuel distribution, adding a whole new subsystem that injects much more fuel throughout the combustion sequence to develop radically greater thrust.

WINNING, SEBULBA STYLE

Sebulba is maniacally driven to win, and his determination goes farther than exceeding race rules on his engine parameters and threatening race officials who ask too many questions. Whispered rumours in the pits describe weapons built into Sebulba's engines. At the 800 kph (500 mph) speeds of Podracing, who can tell what's really happening way out there on the flats and in the canyons? So far his crimes go unpunished. Sebulba has been accused before, but his engines always seem to be clean when officials demand an inspection. Different systems made to be removable keep the wily Dug from being caught for his murderous cheating. At present, his primary weapon is a flame emitter, which fries competitors' engines.

Telemetry and control console

Sebulba

Control power generator

Control linkage

The telemetry computers of the Podracer cockpit must withstand race conditions while calculating ideal pressure/temperature algorithms and organizing the information flowing from the engine telemetry sensors

Anakin Skywalker

Throttle levers

Air scoops

Control pod

The interlinked cockpit computer parts require a special power cell that delivers a high-voltage filtered electronic power feed to the computers

Fuel injector ring

Tri-carbon anti-turbulence vanes

Control linkage

Combustion chamber and direct variable air inlet

Steelton control cable

Thrust stabilizer cone

Thrust ring

Fuel lines

Spill air doors

Fuel injector nozzles

Core fuel tank

8-stage main compressor

Mini-acceleration compensator

Repulsorlift generator

Afterburner heat dissipator fins

Flame emitter weapon

Energy binder plate

Fuel atomizer/ distributors

SIZE AND PERFORMANCE

Most Podracers go for greater power through greater size, exploiting loopholes in the racing rules to enter larger and more powerful engines with tacked-on subsystems to increase their performance. Sebulba's engines are barely within the rules and would probably not hold up to close inspection, but the race referees know better than to press the issue too hard with the evil Dug. Anakin's engines are remarkable in that he has derived incredible performance from engines smaller than everything else currently used. It all comes from his radical fuel atomizer and distribution system, with multiple igniters throughout the system to get maximum burn from every atom of fuel. In effect the whole engine is an afterburner once it gets going, but the system works on extremely delicate balances and can be flooded with fuel if pushed before the engines are going full bore, as Anakin finds out early on.

Turbine drive motor

Turbine drive energizer

Primary intake turbine

Triple air scoops

ANAKIN'S & SEBULBA'S PODRACERS

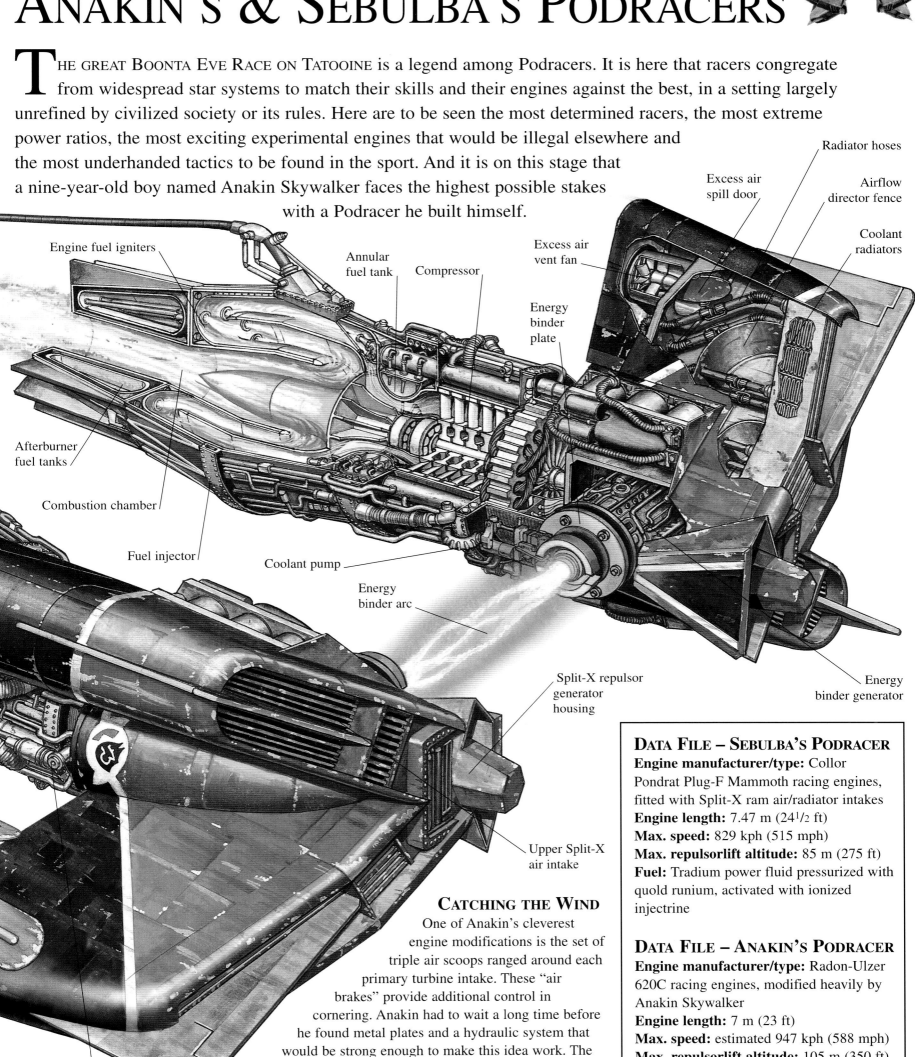

THE GREAT BOONTA EVE RACE ON TATOOINE is a legend among Podracers. It is here that racers congregate from widespread star systems to match their skills and their engines against the best, in a setting largely unrefined by civilized society or its rules. Here are to be seen the most determined racers, the most extreme power ratios, the most exciting experimental engines that would be illegal elsewhere and the most underhanded tactics to be found in the sport. And it is on this stage that a nine-year-old boy named Anakin Skywalker faces the highest possible stakes with a Podracer he built himself.

Engine fuel igniters

Annular fuel tank

Compressor

Excess air vent fan

Energy binder plate

Radiator hoses

Excess air spill door

Airflow director fence

Coolant radiators

Afterburner fuel tanks

Combustion chamber

Fuel injector

Coolant pump

Energy binder arc

Energy binder generator

Split-X repulsor generator housing

Upper Split-X air intake

Over-pressure system valve

Split-X stabilizing vane

CATCHING THE WIND

One of Anakin's cleverest engine modifications is the set of triple air scoops ranged around each primary turbine intake. These "air brakes" provide additional control in cornering. Anakin had to wait a long time before he found metal plates and a hydraulic system that would be strong enough to make this idea work. The hydraulic struts are of Tyrian manufacture and came from a military surplus lot that Watto bought from Dreddon the Hutt, a crimelord known to make many arms deals in the star systems of the Outer Rim.

DATA FILE – SEBULBA'S PODRACER
Engine manufacturer/type: Collor Pondrat Plug-F Mammoth racing engines, fitted with Split-X ram air/radiator intakes
Engine length: 7.47 m (24$\frac{1}{2}$ ft)
Max. speed: 829 kph (515 mph)
Max. repulsorlift altitude: 85 m (275 ft)
Fuel: Tradium power fluid pressurized with quold runium, activated with ionized injectrine

DATA FILE – ANAKIN'S PODRACER
Engine manufacturer/type: Radon-Ulzer 620C racing engines, modified heavily by Anakin Skywalker
Engine length: 7 m (23 ft)
Max. speed: estimated 947 kph (588 mph)
Max. repulsorlift altitude: 105 m (350 ft)
Fuel: straight Tradium power fluid activated with injectrine, no additives

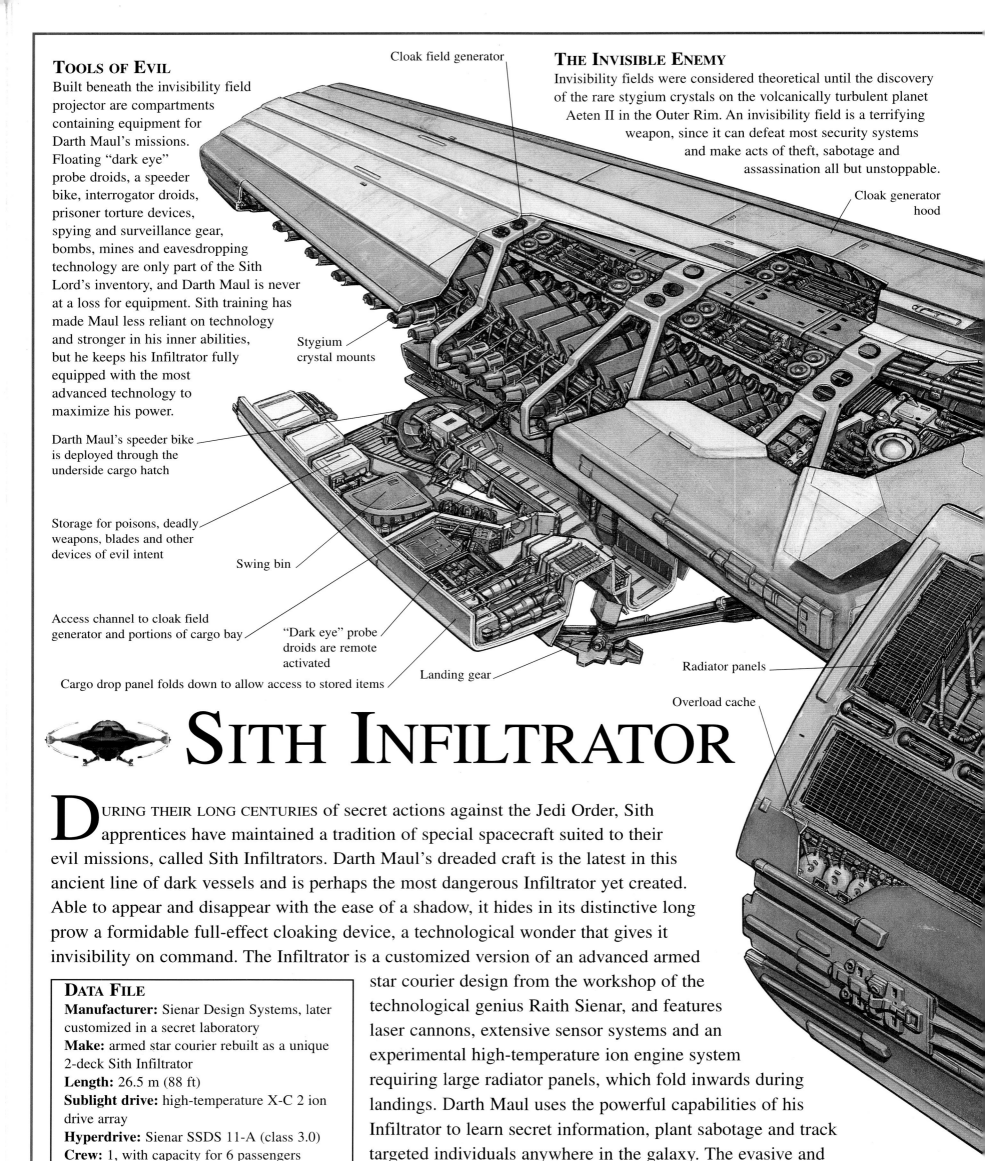

TOOLS OF EVIL

Built beneath the invisibility field projector are compartments containing equipment for Darth Maul's missions. Floating "dark eye" probe droids, a speeder bike, interrogator droids, prisoner torture devices, spying and surveillance gear, bombs, mines and eavesdropping technology are only part of the Sith Lord's inventory, and Darth Maul is never at a loss for equipment. Sith training has made Maul less reliant on technology and stronger in his inner abilities, but he keeps his Infiltrator fully equipped with the most advanced technology to maximize his power.

Darth Maul's speeder bike is deployed through the underside cargo hatch

Storage for poisons, deadly weapons, blades and other devices of evil intent

Access channel to cloak field generator and portions of cargo bay

Cargo drop panel folds down to allow access to stored items

Cloak field generator

Stygium crystal mounts

Swing bin

"Dark eye" probe droids are remote activated

Landing gear

THE INVISIBLE ENEMY

Invisibility fields were considered theoretical until the discovery of the rare stygium crystals on the volcanically turbulent planet Aeten II in the Outer Rim. An invisibility field is a terrifying weapon, since it can defeat most security systems and make acts of theft, sabotage and assassination all but unstoppable.

Cloak generator hood

Radiator panels

Overload cache

SITH INFILTRATOR

DURING THEIR LONG CENTURIES of secret actions against the Jedi Order, Sith apprentices have maintained a tradition of special spacecraft suited to their evil missions, called Sith Infiltrators. Darth Maul's dreaded craft is the latest in this ancient line of dark vessels and is perhaps the most dangerous Infiltrator yet created. Able to appear and disappear with the ease of a shadow, it hides in its distinctive long prow a formidable full-effect cloaking device, a technological wonder that gives it invisibility on command. The Infiltrator is a customized version of an advanced armed star courier design from the workshop of the technological genius Raith Sienar, and features laser cannons, extensive sensor systems and an experimental high-temperature ion engine system requiring large radiator panels, which fold inwards during landings. Darth Maul uses the powerful capabilities of his Infiltrator to learn secret information, plant sabotage and track targeted individuals anywhere in the galaxy. The evasive and deadly craft is an appropriate extension of the uncanny abilities of its Sith Lord pilot.

DATA FILE

Manufacturer: Sienar Design Systems, later customized in a secret laboratory
Make: armed star courier rebuilt as a unique 2-deck Sith Infiltrator
Length: 26.5 m (88 ft)
Sublight drive: high-temperature X-C 2 ion drive array
Hyperdrive: Sienar SSDS 11-A (class 3.0)
Crew: 1, with capacity for 6 passengers
Primary armament: 6 low-profile laser cannons (4 original, 2 added)

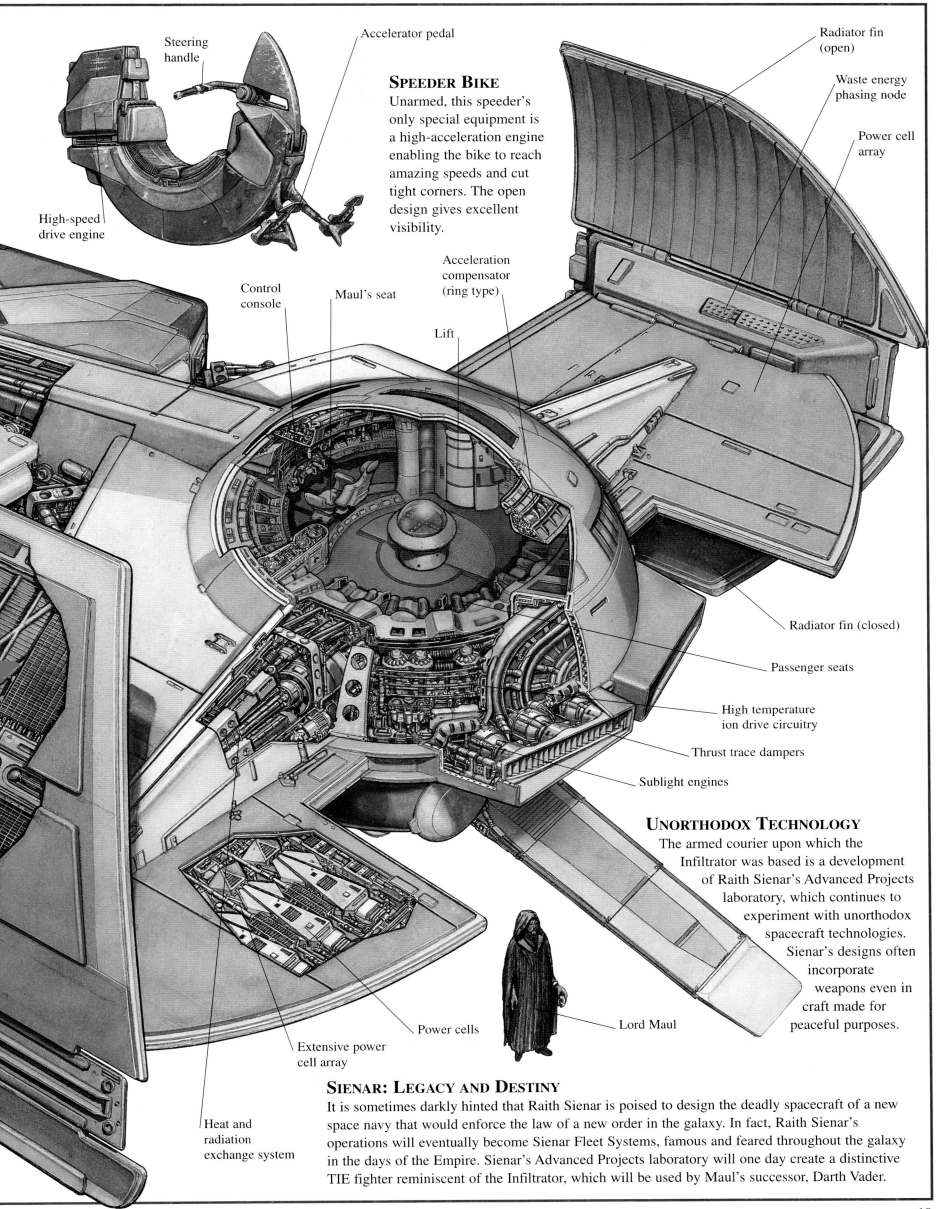

Steering
handle

Accelerator pedal

High-speed
drive engine

SPEEDER BIKE
Unarmed, this speeder's
only special equipment is
a high-acceleration engine
enabling the bike to reach
amazing speeds and cut
tight corners. The open
design gives excellent
visibility.

Control
console

Maul's seat

Acceleration
compensator
(ring type)

Lift

Radiator fin
(open)

Waste energy
phasing node

Power cell
array

Radiator fin (closed)

Passenger seats

High temperature
ion drive circuitry

Thrust trace dampers

Sublight engines

UNORTHODOX TECHNOLOGY
The armed courier upon which the
Infiltrator was based is a development
of Raith Sienar's Advanced Projects
laboratory, which continues to
experiment with unorthodox
spacecraft technologies.
Sienar's designs often
incorporate
weapons even in
craft made for
peaceful purposes.

Power cells

Extensive power
cell array

Lord Maul

Heat and
radiation
exchange system

SIENAR: LEGACY AND DESTINY
It is sometimes darkly hinted that Raith Sienar is poised to design the deadly spacecraft of a new
space navy that would enforce the law of a new order in the galaxy. In fact, Raith Sienar's
operations will eventually become Sienar Fleet Systems, famous and feared throughout the galaxy
in the days of the Empire. Sienar's Advanced Projects laboratory will one day create a distinctive
TIE fighter reminiscent of the Infiltrator, which will be used by Maul's successor, Darth Vader.

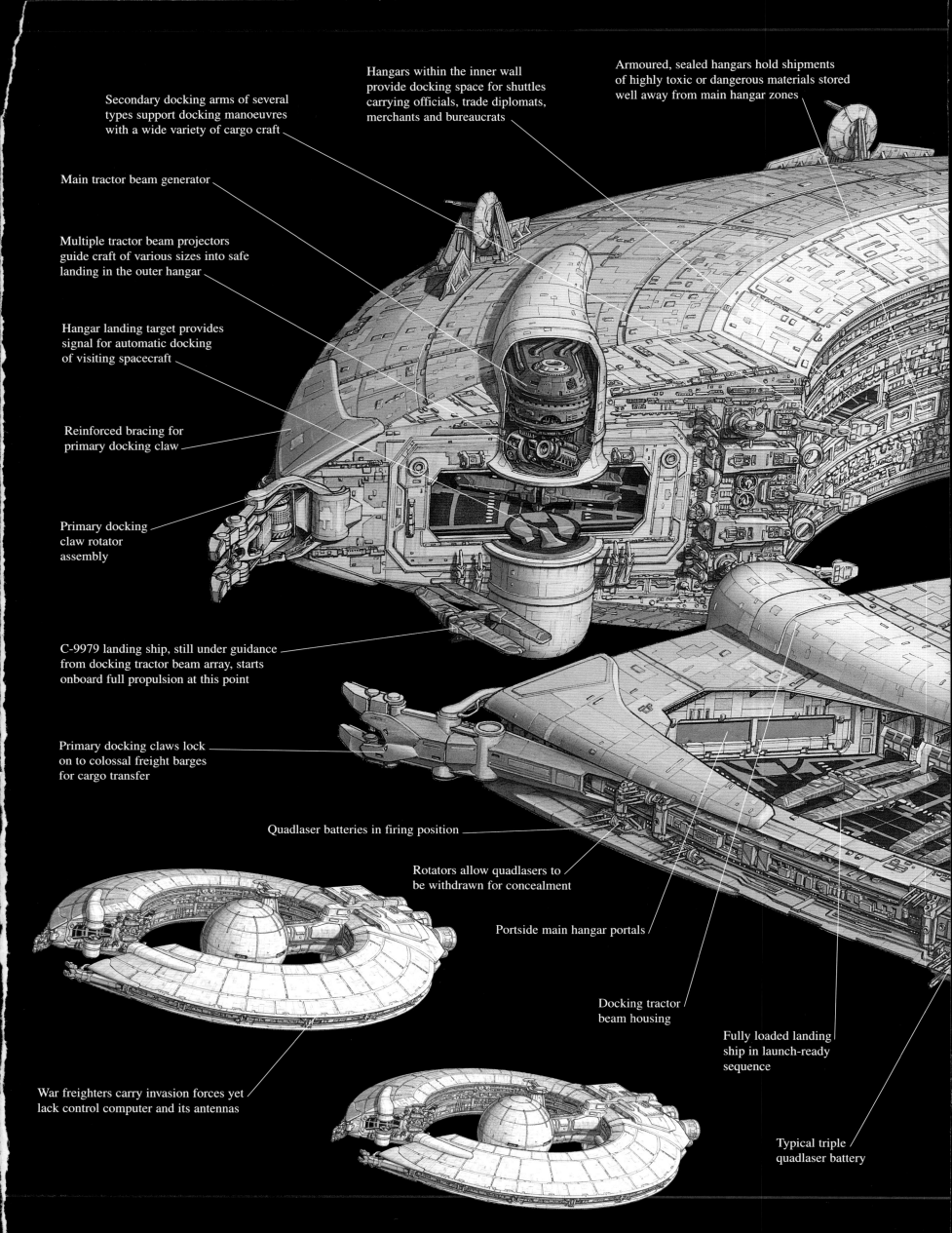

Secondary docking arms of several types support docking manoeuvres with a wide variety of cargo craft

Hangars within the inner wall provide docking space for shuttles carrying officials, trade diplomats, merchants and bureaucrats

Armoured, sealed hangars hold shipments of highly toxic or dangerous materials stored well away from main hangar zones

Main tractor beam generator

Multiple tractor beam projectors guide craft of various sizes into safe landing in the outer hangar

Hangar landing target provides signal for automatic docking of visiting spacecraft

Reinforced bracing for primary docking claw

Primary docking claw rotator assembly

C-9979 landing ship, still under guidance from docking tractor beam array, starts onboard full propulsion at this point

Primary docking claws lock on to colossal freight barges for cargo transfer

Quadlaser batteries in firing position

Rotators allow quadlasers to be withdrawn for concealment

Portside main hangar portals

Docking tractor beam housing

Fully loaded landing ship in launch-ready sequence

War freighters carry invasion forces yet lack control computer and its antennas

Typical triple quadlaser battery

Droid Control Ship

Frstage the very first stages of planning to build their secret army, the Trade Federation armaments committee had in mind the use of their great commercial fleet of giant cargo ships for transporting the weapons of war. Familiar to millions of officials and civilian personnel who dealt with them over the skies of numerous planets, the characteristic giant Trade Federation cargo ships had been built over many years, plying cargo among the far-flung stars of the galaxy as part of the extensive market of the Trade Federation. These seemingly harmless and slow-moving container ships would now hide, deep within their hangars, the tremendous army built to change the rules of commerce. Upon the first complete council approval of the secret army plan, the cargo fleet was brought under study, and by the end of the project's construction phase the Neimoidians had created from them a frightening fleet of battleships.

War Conversions

The converted battleships bear unusual equipment for cargo freighters, including powerful quadlaser batteries designed to destroy opposition fighters launched against the secret army transports. These batteries are built to rotate inwards while not in use, concealing their true nature until the Neimoidians wish to uncloak their military intentions to unsuspecting "future customers". While the cargo hangars and their ceiling racks in the inner hangar zones proved sufficient for the carriage of the secret army ground forces, additional large electrified racks were installed in the outermost hangar zones to quarter the dangerous colonies of droid starfighters, which draw power from the racks until launch.

Civilian Compromises

While the Trade Federation cargo fleet was ideal for hiding the existence of the secret army and carrying it unobtrusively to points of deployment, the commercial origins of the battleships leave them with shortcomings as "battleships". Fitted with numerous guns around the equatorial bands, the battleships carry considerable firepower with very limited coverage and so large areas of the ship are undefended by emplaced artillery. The onboard swarms of droid starfighters are thus essential for defence of the battleships from fighter attack.

Tractor array power system

Hull strengthened with irregular armour plating

Starboard hangar arm

Scanner array

Giant acceleration compensator prevents acceleration damage

Primary drive engines

Centresphere

Secondary drive engine

The Hand Behind the Secret Army

While the Trade Federation has long been known as a greedy and conniving organization of merchants, the use of armed force to increase their profits hardly seems to suit their fairly cowardly nature. A strange force has been at work within the Trade Federation, making it capable of extraordinary measures and commiting it to a course of conflict and outright war that will shake the very Galactic Republic. At its core, the Trade Federation's secret army appears to be the vision of a shadowy figure called Darth Sidious, who has been manipulating powerful Neimoidians to do his mysterious bidding. The Sith title of this dark lord holds menace for all, and no one can guess where this disturbing course of events will lead.

DROID STARFIGHTER

THE SPACE FIGHTERS deployed from the Trade Federation battleships are themselves droids, not piloted by any living being. Showered upon enemies in tremendous swarms, droid starfighters dart through space in maddening fury, elusive targets and deadly opponents for living defenders. They are controlled by a continuously modulated signal from the central Droid Control Ship computer, which keeps track of every single individual fighter just as it pulses through the processor of every single battle droid. The signal receiver and onboard computer brain is in the "head" of the fighter and twin sensor pits serve as eyes. They are the most sophisticated automated starfighters ever built, carrying four laser cannons as well as two energy torpedo launchers, which pack them with firepower far beyond their size class.

Retracted walk mode claws

Composite shell covers antenna that receives control signal

Thrust exhaust nozzles

Landing repulsor bands

ATTACK AND FLIGHT MODES
To both protect and conceal its deadly laser cannons, the droid starfighter retracts its wings in flight mode (above). In this configuration, the droid can hide its military nature, enabling it to ambush the unwary. Covering the weapons when not in use, shielding them from micro-particles and atmospheric corrosion, can also improve their accuracy by a tiny degree, an effort at high precision typical of the Haor Chall engineer initiates.

Energy torpedo cannon

Thrust exhaust nozzles

Engine module as removed for refuelling

Solid fuel slug chamber

Solid fuel slug

Thrust dampers electromagnetically vector propulsion

Engine cooling fins

Hydraulic wing/leg extension system

Walking leg struts (retracted)

Hydraulic and pneumatic charging systems for wing deployment and leg walking movement

Flight assault lasers

Laser muzzle brake

Antigravity generator

Power converter

Internal system cooling unit and demagnetizer

Light non-magnetic alclad alloy plating

SOLID FIRE FUEL
Unconventional solid fuel concentrate slugs give droid starfighters their powerful thrust. Expensive to manufacture, the slugs burn furiously when ignited, allowing the droid starfighter to hurtle through space with minimal engine mass. Thrust streams are vectored electromagnetically for steering. The solid fuel system limits the droids' fighting time, but the numerous droids are easily recycled back into their racks for recharge and refuelling when spent.

Permanently installed power cells are recharged while droid is locked into war freighter power grid

DATA FILE
Design and manufacture: Xi Char cathedral factories, Charros IV
Length: 3.5 m (12 ft) wing tip to wing tip
Crew: permanent automated droid brain controlled by remote signal
Armament: 4 blaster cannons, 2 energy torpedo launchers
Flight time before refuelling: 35 minutes

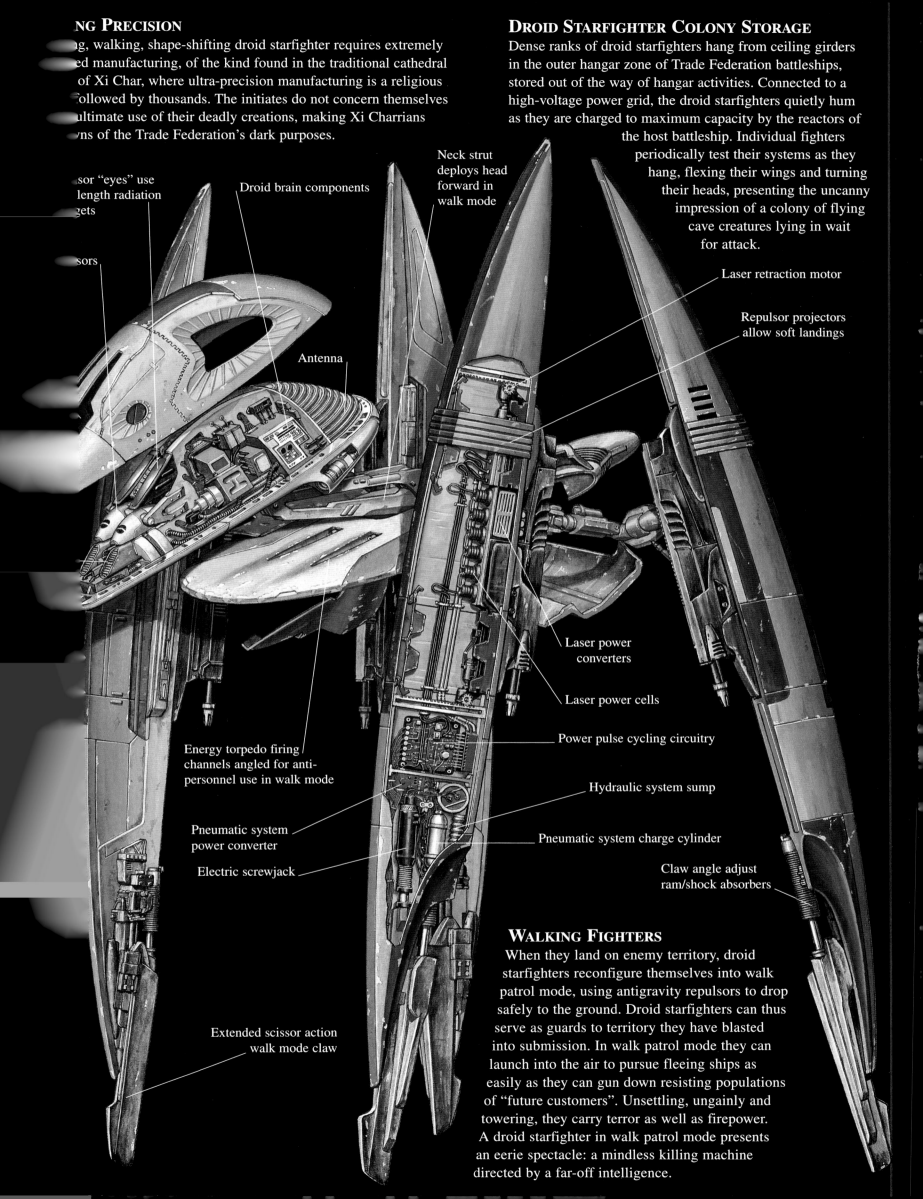

NG PRECISION

...ng, walking, shape-shifting droid starfighter requires extremely
...ed manufacturing, of the kind found in the traditional cathedral
...of Xi Char, where ultra-precision manufacturing is a religious
...followed by thousands. The initiates do not concern themselves
...ultimate use of their deadly creations, making Xi Charrians
...ns of the Trade Federation's dark purposes.

...sor "eyes" use
length radiation
...gets

...sors

Droid brain components

Neck strut
deploys head
forward in
walk mode

Antenna

DROID STARFIGHTER COLONY STORAGE

Dense ranks of droid starfighters hang from ceiling girders
in the outer hangar zone of Trade Federation battleships,
stored out of the way of hangar activities. Connected to a
high-voltage power grid, the droid starfighters quietly hum
as they are charged to maximum capacity by the reactors of
the host battleship. Individual fighters
periodically test their systems as they
hang, flexing their wings and turning
their heads, presenting the uncanny
impression of a colony of flying
cave creatures lying in wait
for attack.

Laser retraction motor

Repulsor projectors
allow soft landings

Laser power
converters

Laser power cells

Energy torpedo firing
channels angled for anti-
personnel use in walk mode

Power pulse cycling circuitry

Hydraulic system sump

Pneumatic system
power converter

Pneumatic system charge cylinder

Electric screwjack

Claw angle adjust
ram/shock absorbers

WALKING FIGHTERS

When they land on enemy territory, droid
starfighters reconfigure themselves into walk
patrol mode, using antigravity repulsors to drop
safely to the ground. Droid starfighters can thus
serve as guards to territory they have blasted
into submission. In walk patrol mode they can
launch into the air to pursue fleeing ships as
easily as they can gun down resisting populations
of "future customers". Unsettling, ungainly and
towering, they carry terror as well as firepower.
A droid starfighter in walk patrol mode presents
an eerie spectacle: a mindless killing machine
directed by a far-off intelligence.

Extended scissor action
walk mode claw

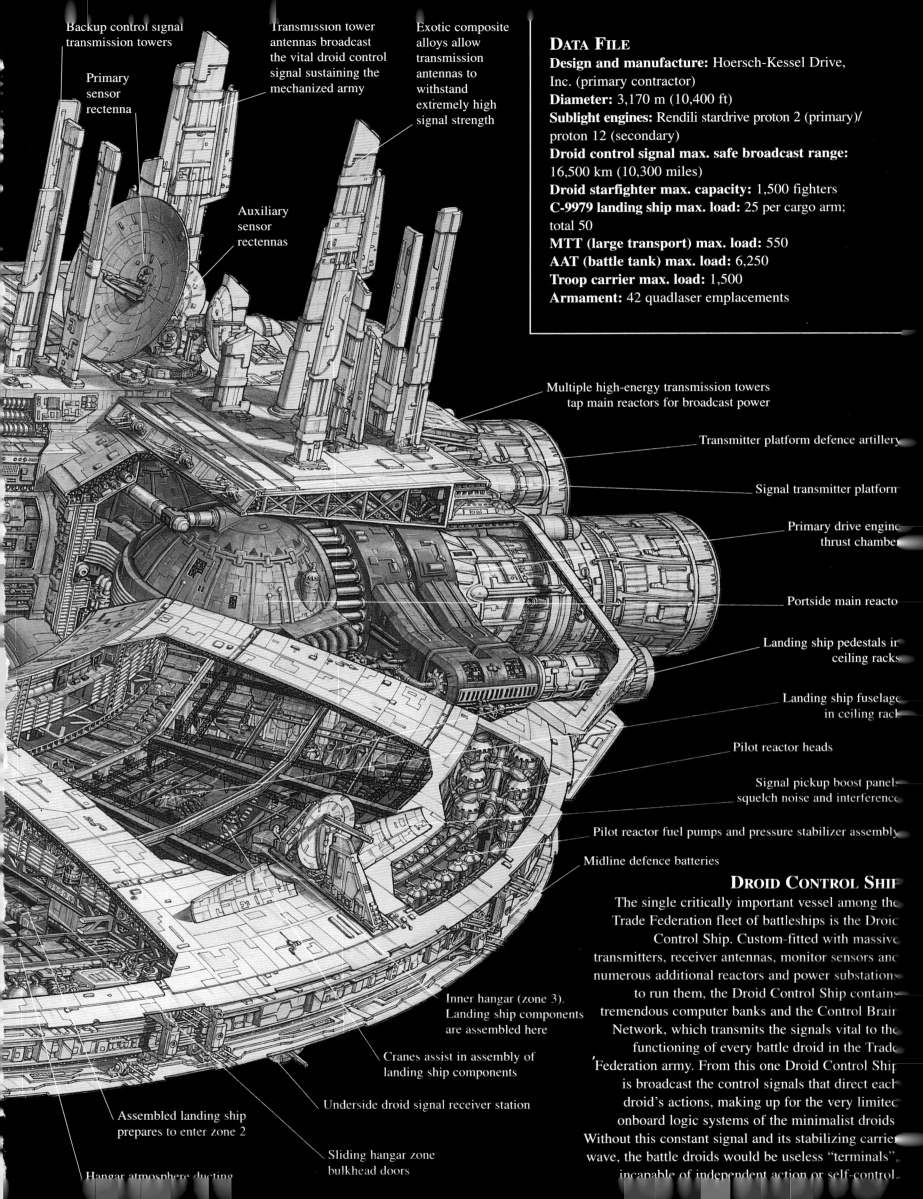

Backup control signal transmission towers

Primary sensor rectenna

Transmission tower antennas broadcast the vital droid control signal sustaining the mechanized army

Exotic composite alloys allow transmission antennas to withstand extremely high signal strength

Auxiliary sensor rectennas

DATA FILE

Design and manufacture: Hoersch-Kessel Drive, Inc. (primary contractor)
Diameter: 3,170 m (10,400 ft)
Sublight engines: Rendili stardrive proton 2 (primary)/ proton 12 (secondary)
Droid control signal max. safe broadcast range: 16,500 km (10,300 miles)
Droid starfighter max. capacity: 1,500 fighters
C-9979 landing ship max. load: 25 per cargo arm; total 50
MTT (large transport) max. load: 550
AAT (battle tank) max. load: 6,250
Troop carrier max. load: 1,500
Armament: 42 quadlaser emplacements

Multiple high-energy transmission towers tap main reactors for broadcast power

Transmitter platform defence artillery

Signal transmitter platform

Primary drive engine thrust chamber

Portside main reactor

Landing ship pedestals in ceiling racks

Landing ship fuselage in ceiling rack

Pilot reactor heads

Signal pickup boost panels squelch noise and interference

Pilot reactor fuel pumps and pressure stabilizer assembly

Midline defence batteries

DROID CONTROL SHIP

The single critically important vessel among the Trade Federation fleet of battleships is the Droid Control Ship. Custom-fitted with massive transmitters, receiver antennas, monitor sensors and numerous additional reactors and power substations to run them, the Droid Control Ship contains tremendous computer banks and the Control Brain Network, which transmits the signals vital to the functioning of every battle droid in the Trade Federation army. From this one Droid Control Ship is broadcast the control signals that direct each droid's actions, making up for the very limited onboard logic systems of the minimalist droids. Without this constant signal and its stabilizing carrier wave, the battle droids would be useless "terminals", incapable of independent action or self-control.

Inner hangar (zone 3). Landing ship components are assembled here

Cranes assist in assembly of landing ship components

Underside droid signal receiver station

Assembled landing ship prepares to enter zone 2

Sliding hangar zone bulkhead doors

Hangar atmosphere ducting

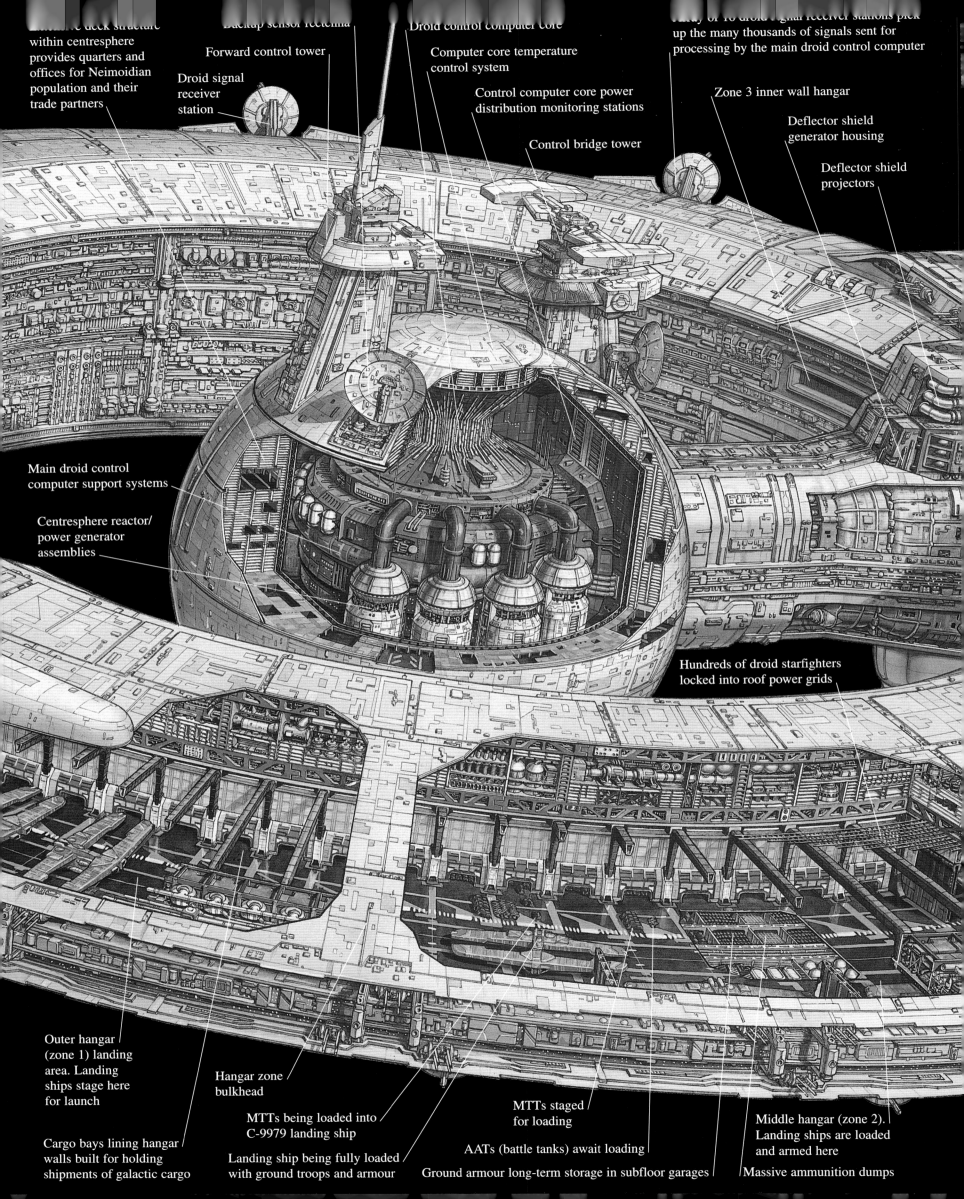

Inferitive deck structure within centresphere provides quarters and offices for Neimoidian population and their trade partners

Backup sensor rectenna

Droid control computer core

Party of 16 droid signal receiver stations pick up the many thousands of signals sent for processing by the main droid control computer

Forward control tower

Computer core temperature control system

Droid signal receiver station

Control computer core power distribution monitoring stations

Zone 3 inner wall hangar

Deflector shield generator housing

Control bridge tower

Deflector shield projectors

Main droid control computer support systems

Centresphere reactor/ power generator assemblies

Hundreds of droid starfighters locked into roof power grids

Outer hangar (zone 1) landing area. Landing ships stage here for launch

Hangar zone bulkhead

MTTs staged for loading

Middle hangar (zone 2). Landing ships are loaded and armed here

Cargo bays lining hangar walls built for holding shipments of galactic cargo

MTTs being loaded into C-9979 landing ship

AATs (battle tanks) await loading

Landing ship being fully loaded with ground troops and armour

Ground armour long-term storage in subfloor garages

Massive ammunition dumps

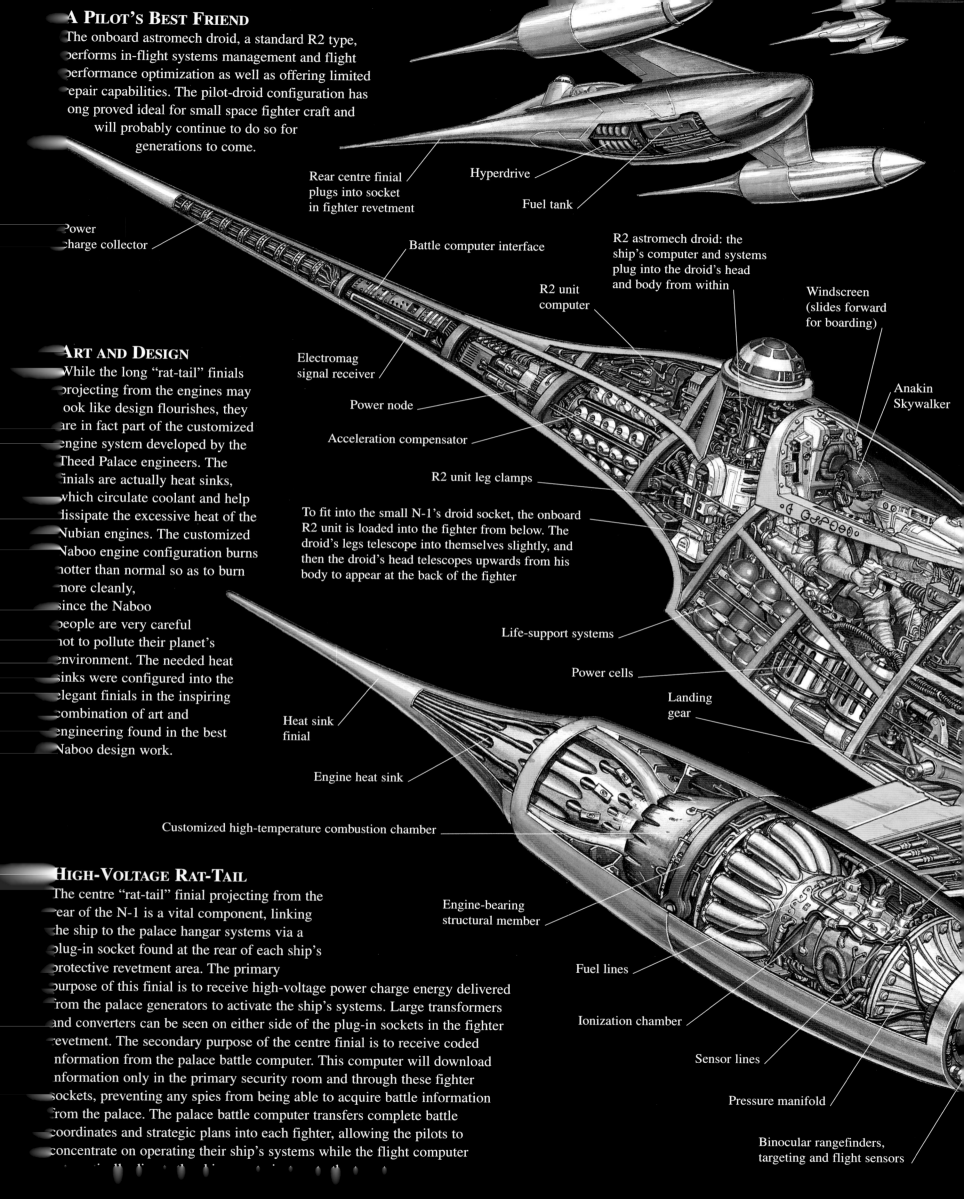

A PILOT'S BEST FRIEND

The onboard astromech droid, a standard R2 type, performs in-flight systems management and flight performance optimization as well as offering limited repair capabilities. The pilot-droid configuration has long proved ideal for small space fighter craft and will probably continue to do so for generations to come.

Rear centre finial plugs into socket in fighter revetment

Hyperdrive

Fuel tank

Power charge collector

Battle computer interface

R2 astromech droid: the ship's computer and systems plug into the droid's head and body from within

Windscreen (slides forward for boarding)

R2 unit computer

Electromag signal receiver

Anakin Skywalker

ART AND DESIGN

While the long "rat-tail" finials projecting from the engines may look like design flourishes, they are in fact part of the customized engine system developed by the Theed Palace engineers. The finials are actually heat sinks, which circulate coolant and help dissipate the excessive heat of the Nubian engines. The customized Naboo engine configuration burns hotter than normal so as to burn more cleanly, since the Naboo people are very careful not to pollute their planet's environment. The needed heat sinks were configured into the elegant finials in the inspiring combination of art and engineering found in the best Naboo design work.

Power node

Acceleration compensator

R2 unit leg clamps

To fit into the small N-1's droid socket, the onboard R2 unit is loaded into the fighter from below. The droid's legs telescope into themselves slightly, and then the droid's head telescopes upwards from his body to appear at the back of the fighter

Life-support systems

Power cells

Landing gear

Heat sink finial

Engine heat sink

Customized high-temperature combustion chamber

HIGH-VOLTAGE RAT-TAIL

The centre "rat-tail" finial projecting from the rear of the N-1 is a vital component, linking the ship to the palace hangar systems via a plug-in socket found at the rear of each ship's protective revetment area. The primary purpose of this finial is to receive high-voltage power charge energy delivered from the palace generators to activate the ship's systems. Large transformers and converters can be seen on either side of the plug-in sockets in the fighter revetment. The secondary purpose of the centre finial is to receive coded information from the palace battle computer. This computer will download information only in the primary security room and through these fighter sockets, preventing any spies from being able to acquire battle information from the palace. The palace battle computer transfers complete battle coordinates and strategic plans into each fighter, allowing the pilots to concentrate on operating their ship's systems while the flight computer

Engine-bearing structural member

Fuel lines

Ionization chamber

Sensor lines

Pressure manifold

Binocular rangefinders, targeting and flight sensors

NABOO N-1 STARFIGHTER

T HE SINGLE PILOT NABOO ROYAL N-1 STARFIGHTER was developed by the Theed Palace Space Vessel Engineering Corps for the volunteer Royal Naboo Security Forces. Sleek and agile, the small N-1 faces aggressors with twin blaster cannons and a double magazine of proton torpedoes. Found only on Naboo and rarely seen even there, the N-1, like the Queen's Royal Starship, uses many standard galactic internal components in a custom-built spaceframe that reflects the Naboo people's love of handcrafted, elegant shapes. The Naboo engineers fabricate some of their own parts such as fuel tanks and sensor antennas, but most of the high-technology gear is acquired through trade from other, more industrialized worlds. The Theed Palace engineers developed a customized engine system, however, based on a standard Nubian drive motor but modified significantly to release fewer emissions into the atmosphere. The Naboo being a peaceful people, the Space Fighter Corps is maintained as much through tradition as for military defence, and primarily serves as an honour guard for the Queen's Royal Starship. Nonetheless, the Royal Naboo Security Forces train in the N-1s on a regular basis, prepared for the honour of serving the Queen in combat if necessary, since service to the Queen symbolizes service to the great free people of Naboo themselves.

THAT GLEAMING ROYAL LOOK

The N-1 fighter sports a gleaming chromium finish on its forward surfaces. Purely decorative, this finish indicates the ship's royal allegiance. Early Naboo spacecraft required a chrome-like finish for protection from harmful rays in the planet's upper atmosphere. Now that spacecraft and their pilots are fully shielded from such rays by electromagnetic field technology, the chrome finish is retained for tradition and kept as a royal symbol. Only royal ships may carry the hand-finished royal chromium treatment.

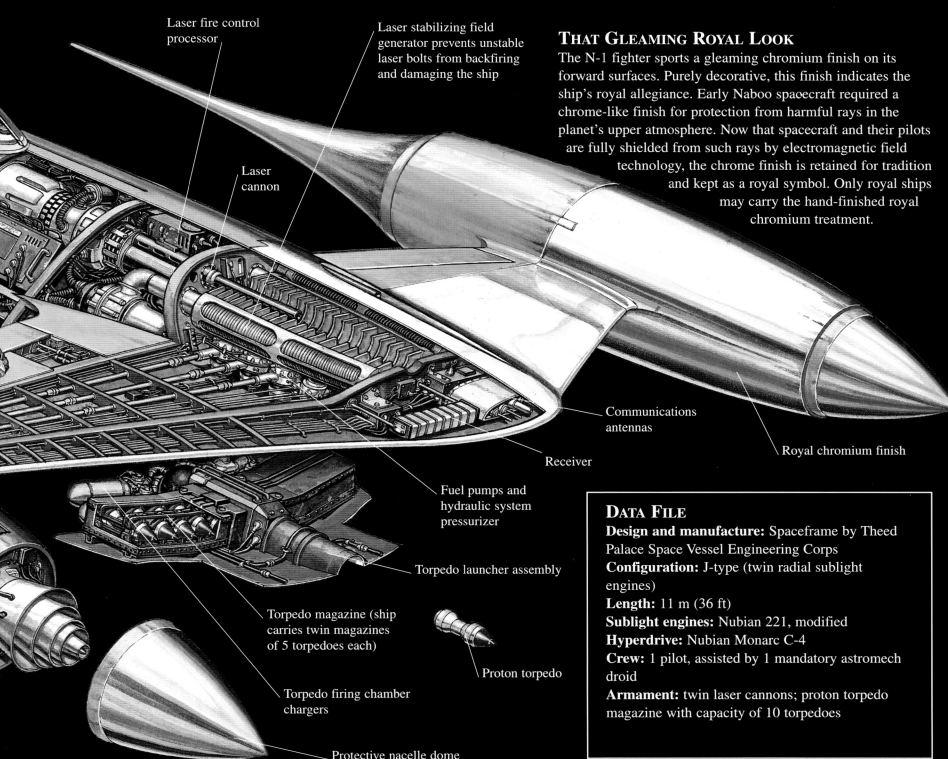

Laser fire control processor

Laser stabilizing field generator prevents unstable laser bolts from backfiring and damaging the ship

Laser cannon

Communications antennas

Receiver

Royal chromium finish

Fuel pumps and hydraulic system pressurizer

Torpedo launcher assembly

Torpedo magazine (ship carries twin magazines of 5 torpedoes each)

Proton torpedo

Torpedo firing chamber chargers

Protective nacelle dome

DATA FILE

Design and manufacture: Spaceframe by Theed Palace Space Vessel Engineering Corps
Configuration: J-type (twin radial sublight engines)
Length: 11 m (36 ft)
Sublight engines: Nubian 221, modified
Hyperdrive: Nubian Monarc C-4
Crew: 1 pilot, assisted by 1 mandatory astromech droid
Armament: twin laser cannons; proton torpedo magazine with capacity of 10 torpedoes

AAT (BATTLE TANK)

DESIGNED AND BUILT by the Baktoid Armour Workshop for the Trade Federation secret army, the AAT (battle tank) carries a crew of four battle droids into combat, presenting the enemy with a heavily armoured facade and a blistering hail of assault fire from five laser guns and six energy shell launchers. Their deployment on Naboo is their first use in open combat, but the tanks have seen considerable training action, leaving them scarred and weathered. The AAT is designed for head-on combat in formal battle lines and is accordingly very heavily armoured up front. In fact, the nose of the AAT is almost solid armour, designed to crash through heavy walls with impunity.

Rangefinders

Laser charge battery

Secondary laser guns

INSIDE THE COCKPIT

A droid pilot guides the AAT and provides targeting information to the two gunners. The pilot uses a stereoscopic camera which relays information into a periscope scanner.

Primary laser cannon

Up to 6 ground troop battle droids can ride into battle using the 3 handholds on either side of the tank body

Front hatch: pilot can open it for direct visual sighting if camera damaged

AAT pilot

Auxiliary status read-outs

DATA FILE
Design and manufacture: Baktoid Armour Workshop
Make: AAT (Armoured Assault Tank)
Length: 9.75 m (32 ft)
Max. speed: 55 kph (35 mph)
Crew: 4 battle droids (commander, pilot, 2 gunners)
Armament: primary turret laser cannon; twin lateral range-finding lasers; twin lateral anti-personnel lasers; 6 energy shell projectile launchers

Short range blaster

Air cooling intake

Rocket launcher armour plate

Nose ram

Heavy solid plate armour

Forward repulsor disc

Bunker-busting shells

Armour-piercing shells

Energy cocooning chamber

Launch tube

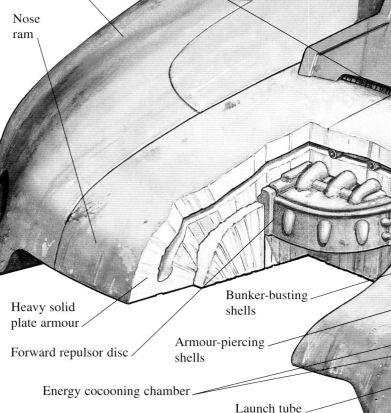

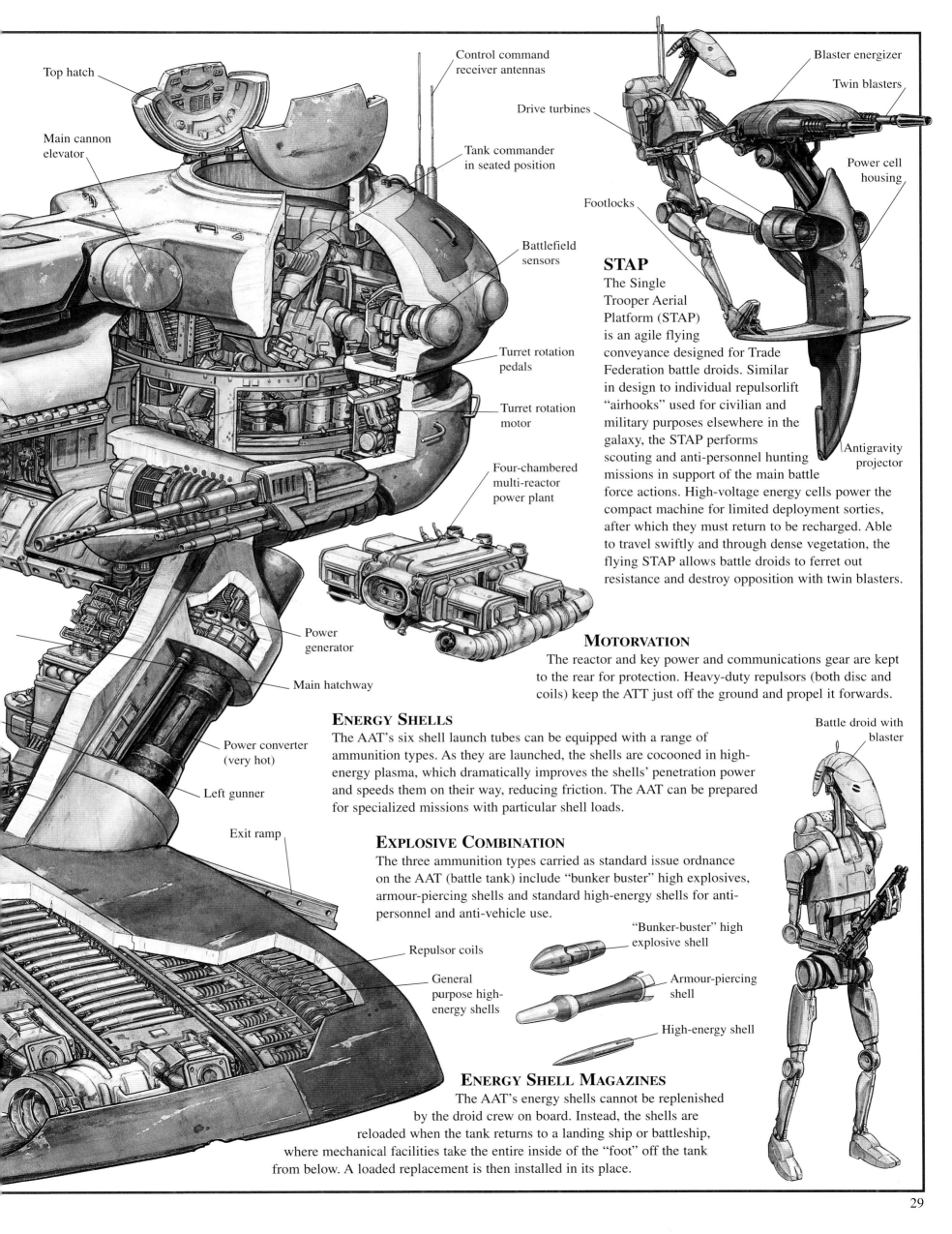

Top hatch

Main cannon
elevator

Control command
receiver antennas

Drive turbines

Blaster energizer

Twin blasters

Tank commander
in seated position

Footlocks

Power cell
housing

Battlefield
sensors

Turret rotation
pedals

Turret rotation
motor

Four-chambered
multi-reactor
power plant

Power
generator

Main hatchway

Power converter
(very hot)

Left gunner

Exit ramp

Repulsor coils

General
purpose high-
energy shells

STAP

The Single Trooper Aerial Platform (STAP) is an agile flying conveyance designed for Trade Federation battle droids. Similar in design to individual repulsorlift "airhooks" used for civilian and military purposes elsewhere in the galaxy, the STAP performs scouting and anti-personnel hunting missions in support of the main battle force actions. High-voltage energy cells power the compact machine for limited deployment sorties, after which they must return to be recharged. Able to travel swiftly and through dense vegetation, the flying STAP allows battle droids to ferret out resistance and destroy opposition with twin blasters.

Antigravity
projector

MOTORVATION

The reactor and key power and communications gear are kept to the rear for protection. Heavy-duty repulsors (both disc and coils) keep the ATT just off the ground and propel it forwards.

Battle droid with
blaster

ENERGY SHELLS

The AAT's six shell launch tubes can be equipped with a range of ammunition types. As they are launched, the shells are cocooned in high-energy plasma, which dramatically improves the shells' penetration power and speeds them on their way, reducing friction. The AAT can be prepared for specialized missions with particular shell loads.

EXPLOSIVE COMBINATION

The three ammunition types carried as standard issue ordnance on the AAT (battle tank) include "bunker buster" high explosives, armour-piercing shells and standard high-energy shells for anti-personnel and anti-vehicle use.

"Bunker-buster" high
explosive shell

Armour-piercing
shell

High-energy shell

ENERGY SHELL MAGAZINES

The AAT's energy shells cannot be replenished by the droid crew on board. Instead, the shells are reloaded when the tank returns to a landing ship or battleship, where mechanical facilities take the entire inside of the "foot" off the tank from below. A loaded replacement is then installed in its place.

NABOO SPEEDERS

T HE SMALL GROUND CRAFT of the Naboo Royal Security volunteers are only lightly armed and armoured, since they patrol a fairly peaceful society. They are designed for rapid pursuit and capture of troublemakers rather than combat with an armed enemy. The Flash and Gian speeders are the most common Naboo ground security craft, both vehicles bearing mounts for laser weapons which are sent into action only when such force is absolutely necessary. The Flash speeder is an agile general-use craft with thrust engines finely tuned to give the pilot good control on narrow city streets. The Gian speeder is a heavier and less manoeuvrable vehicle, which is used for forays outside the cities against more serious foes. Extra underside plating protects the Gian speeder from unexpected land mines and rugged ground obstacles.

DATA FILE – FLASH SPEEDER
Length: 4.5 m (14$^{1}/_{2}$ ft)
Crew: 1
Passengers: 1
Armament: 1 laser blaster

DATA FILE – GIAN SPEEDER
Length: 5.7 m (18$^{1}/_{2}$ ft)
Crew: 1 pilot, 1 gunner
Passengers: 2
Armament: 3 laser blasters

FLASH SPEEDERS
One of several small ground vehicles used by the Royal Naboo Security Forces, the Flash landspeeder serves for street patrol and high-speed pursuit of malefactors. The craft normally flies less than a metre off the ground and at maximum can attain a "float" of a couple of metres, but no more is necessary on the paved streets and level grasslands of Naboo. Only slightly modified from the civilian model of the Flash speeder, the craft is nonetheless patrol-grade and built of reliable and sturdy construction.

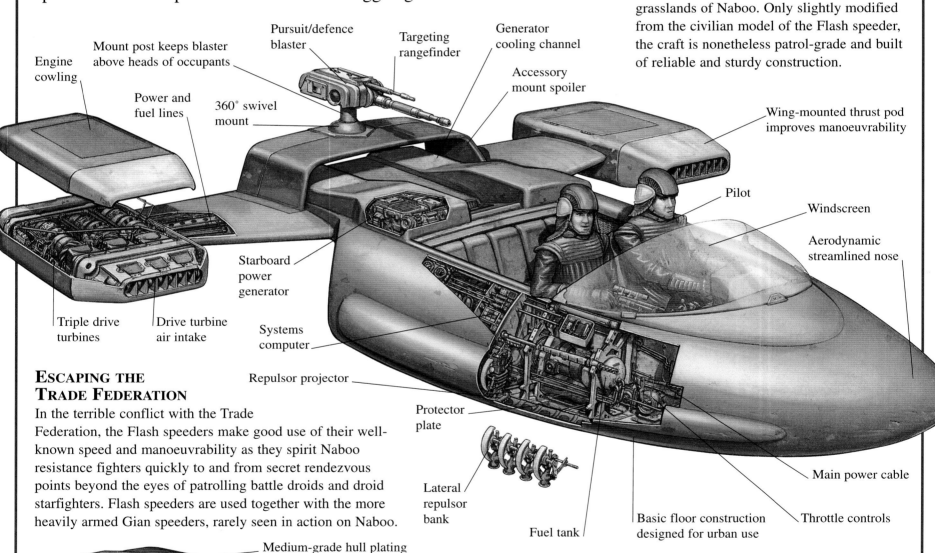

Engine cowling

Mount post keeps blaster above heads of occupants

Pursuit/defence blaster

Targeting rangefinder

Generator cooling channel

Accessory mount spoiler

Power and fuel lines

360° swivel mount

Wing-mounted thrust pod improves manoeuvrability

Pilot

Windscreen

Aerodynamic streamlined nose

Starboard power generator

Triple drive turbines

Drive turbine air intake

Systems computer

Repulsor projector

Protector plate

Lateral repulsor bank

Fuel tank

Basic floor construction designed for urban use

Main power cable

Throttle controls

ESCAPING THE TRADE FEDERATION
In the terrible conflict with the Trade Federation, the Flash speeders make good use of their well-known speed and manoeuvrability as they spirit Naboo resistance fighters quickly to and from secret rendezvous points beyond the eyes of patrolling battle droids and droid starfighters. Flash speeders are used together with the more heavily armed Gian speeders, rarely seen in action on Naboo.

Medium-grade hull plating

Seating for two observers or specialists

Pilot

Thrust pods tucked in to reduce target silhouette

Gunner

Laser generator/ capacitor assembly

Light repeater laser blaster

Auxiliary power unit for each gun

GIAN SPEEDERS
The Gian speeders are heavier vehicles than the Flash speeders and are called out only for serious situations. Their three laser blasters can easily disable non-military vehicles. They have tougher hulls than ordinary civilian craft and their reinforced bodies allow them to withstand glancing hits. Their compact forward silhouette, with thrust pods tucked in behind rather than out on wing struts, makes the Gian less manoeuvrable but a harder target for enemies both in front and behind. To assist in tactical deployments, these speeders can be equipped with customized holographic planning systems.

CORUSCANT TAXI

T HE AIR TAXI SHOOTING THROUGH the vast open spaces between the high skyscrapers is one of the most characteristic sights of the famous metropolis world of Coruscant. These air taxis are allowed unrestricted "free travel" and can thus leave the autonavigating skylanes to take the most direct routes to their destination. Skylanes confine most vehicles on long-distance journeys along defined corridors, without which there would be unmanageable chaos in the air. To rate "free travel", air taxi pilots must pass demanding tests that prove their ability to navigate the unique cityscape with skill and safety. They depend on their scanners, keen eyes and instinct to avoid crashing into other craft, sending passengers plunging into the street canyons far below.

DATA FILE
Length: 8 m (25 ft)
Top speed: 191 kph (115 mph)
Max. altitude: 3.4 km (2.1 miles)
Normal max. trip range: 210 km (131 miles)
Crew: 1
Passengers: depends on species
Armament: none

Communications antenna

Turbine allows rapid acceleration

Forward motion

Efficient drive engine requires a minimum of fuel

Guidance computer balances navigational control between lift repulsors, steering repulsors and drive engines

Luggage can be stored in crossbar compartments

Seats emit mild tractor field in flight to hold passengers securely inside without belts

Headlight circuitry varies spectrum output of beams

Simple construction designed for easy maintenance and repair

Drive engine housing

Multi-spectrum headlights

Side-mounted, low-power repulsors prevent collision and cushion docking

Signal receivers built into body frame pick up air traffic control transmissions

Lift repulsor carries taxi to great skyscraper heights

Precision stabilizing and steering radial repulsor array helps taxi navigate in crowded urban skylanes

WELL-EQUIPPED AIR TAXIS

The standard modern Coruscant air taxi uses a compact, focused, medium-grade repulsor to elevate it to the very highest skyscraper peaks. A radial battery of lower-powered antigravity devices gives it good navigational control in the open air, allowing it to swoop with accuracy around the aerial architecture, docking gently at its final destination. A refined, relatively quiet thrust engine propels the craft with surprising acceleration. Excellent receiver equipment monitors the many channels of Coruscant Air Traffic Control, allowing the pilot to use autonavigation or manual control at any time.

ABOVE AND BELOW

All significant traffic on Coruscant is air traffic – the original ground levels and roads having long ago been abandoned. Sealed tunnels in the lower realms allow for the transport of goods and materials through the city, as bulk shipments are barred by law from the crowded skylanes reserved for travellers.

www.dk.com
A DORLING KINDERSLEY BOOK

PROJECT ART EDITORS Iain Morris, Mark Regardsoe
PROJECT EDITOR David Pickering
EDITORS Joanna Chisholm, Nicholas Turpin
US EDITOR Jane Mason
MANAGING ART EDITOR Cathy Tincknell
DTP DESIGNERS Kim Browne, Jill Bunyan
PRODUCTION Steve Lang

First published in Great Britain in 1999 by
Dorling Kindersley Limited, 9 Henrietta Street, London WC2E 8PS

2 4 6 8 10 9 7 5 3 1

A CIP catalogue record for this book is available from the British Library.

ISBN 0-7513-7058-4

Colour reproduction by Colourscan, Singapore
Printed in Singapore by Tien Wah Press Limited

Acknowledgements
HANS JENSSEN painted the Republic Cruiser, the Trade Federation Landing Ship, Anakin's and Sebulba's Podracers, the Trade Federation Droid Starfighter,
the Trade Federation Droid Control Ship, and the Naboo N-1 Spacefighter.

RICHARD CHASEMORE painted the Trade Federation MTT (large transport), the Gungan Sub, the Naboo Queen's Royal Starship, the Podracers, the Sith
Infiltrator, the Trade Federation AAT (battle tank), the Naboo Speeders, and the Coruscant Taxi.

Hans Jenssen would like to thank Janine Morris and Richard Chasemore would like to thank Hilary Craig for their help and support throughout the project.
The illustrators would also like to thank Kevin Baille for all his invaluable help.

Dorling Kindersley would like to thank Connie Robinson for editorial assistance and Guy Harvey for design assistance.

David Wests Reynolds would like to extend thanks to: Iain Morris, who has proven himself ever more energetic and resourceful on this side of the Atlantic;
Jane Mason, US editor, who kept us on an even keel in yet another venture into wild and uncharted territory; Cara Evangelista, who made sure that quiet
magic occurred to produce vital reference; Tina Mills, who required an entire new office to hold the bursting image files on this project; Christine Owens,
ILM Episode I Image Coordinator, for helping with our many special requests; Nelson Hall and Alexander Ivanov, who specially unveiled and
photographed the treasures of ILM for our reference; Ed "Case" Wright, NAIF Team Technical Staff, Jet Propulsion Laboratory, for special spacecraft
engineering consulting; Concept Designer Doug Chiang, who created the marvelous designs of Episode I and gave us a whole new world to explore with
our cutaway toolkits and whose special involvement has, hopefully, allowed us to offer in this book a true extrapolation of his and George Lucas'
extraordinary Episode I design ideas and concepts; Lucy Wilson and the DK team for putting together another cool project; Ann Marie Reynolds for
keeping me alive all the way to the end; and finally the redoubtable artists Hans "Wig" Jenssen and Richard "Ironhorse" Chasemore, who have developed
the ability to paint things even before they exist. If you've done six impossible things this morning, it's probably fewer than these two have done.
A Captain's salute to one and all.